Split

Split

Lori Weber

James Lorimer & Company Ltd., Publishers
Toronto

© 2005 Lori Weber

James Lorimer & Company Ltd. acknowledges the support of the Ontario Arts Council. We acknowledge the support of the Government of Canada through the Book Publishing Industry Development Program (BPIDP) for our publishing activities. We acknowledge the support of the Canada Council for the Arts for our publishing program. We acknowledge the support of the Government of Ontario through the Ontario Media Development Corporation's Ontario Book Initiative.

 Canada Council   Conseil des Arts
for the Arts   du Canada

ONTARIO ARTS COUNCIL
CONSEIL DES ARTS DE L'ONTARIO

Cover design: Clarke MacDonald

Canada Cataloguing in Publication Data

Weber, Lori, 1959–
  Split / written by Lori Weber

(SideStreets)
ISBN 10: 1-55028-878-4   ISBN 13: 978-1-55028-878-0

I. Title.

PS8645.E24S64 2005   jC813'.6   C2005-900231-X

James Lorimer   Distributed in the United States by:
& Company Ltd.,   Orca Book Publishers,
Publishers   P.O. Box 468
317 Adelaide Street West Custer, WA USA
Suite #1002   98240-0468
Toronto, Ontario
M5V 1P9
www.lorimer.ca

Printed and bound in Canada

For my mom and dad,
Maureen and Wolfgang,
who taught me to love books.

Chapter 1

The sound of a revving motor draws me to the kitchen window, which is covered in spider webs. I look out to see Danny bent over an old car in the back lane, poking around inside the hood. Our massive maple tree droops so low that Danny has to bat its branches out of the way every time he straightens up. The tree is in full foliage now, in the middle of June, and its leaves form a canopy over the back lane. Its huge roots are visible under the poor soil of our yard, like some big monster's claw.

Danny is eighteen, one year older than me. We've known each other for as long as I can remember because we both grew up on this street, just two houses apart. The houses in this neighbourhood are brick triplexes. Each one has an outside staircase winding up to the second floor, then an inside one from there up to the third. Danny and I both live on the ground floor, but we have a triplex sandwiched between us. We used to play together a lot when we were kids, but I haven't seen him for a while. He's wearing a black T-shirt and tight faded jeans and he looks really good.

I go out back through the shed that's attached to our kitchen and stand at the top of the wooden stairs, clutching the rusted wheel of the clothesline. In the yard next door, the white husky circles slowly in the gray dirt, looking for a spot to settle. "Such a pity," my mother always used to say at the sight of Siberia. She'd whistle when she hung out laundry, trying to stimulate the dog, but her efforts rarely earned her more than a whimper.

"Hey, Sandra," Danny calls, coming out from under the hood. Grease spots run up and down his arms like bruises. Aerosmith's "Walk This Way" is blaring on the car radio.

"Hi, Danny. What are you doing?" I call over the music.

"I'm trying to fix this bloody car."

"Where'd you get it?" I ask. "It looks really old."

"Hey, she's only seven. A '71 Monte Carlo. Bought it from some guy in Saint-Jean-sur-Richelieu, when I was there last week."

"What were you doing there?"

"Training for the army," he responds.

"Really? What made you join the army?" I had no idea Danny had done this, not that I necessarily would. It's not like we still hang around.

"A buddy of mine joined last year, so I decided to give it a shot. I mean, what the hell. It was easy to get in. I just had to take a physical where they inspected my vital parts." Danny winks. "Then I had to write a whole bunch of tests to make sure I'm not nuts or anything. But I changed my mind during the training."

"How come?"

"'Cause it was crap! I had to climb ropes and crawl through tires on my belly like a snake. They got me up at the crack of dawn, and I had to stand in lots of lineups and follow a million commands. It was driving me crazy. Too much like Boy Scouts."

"Sounds like Brownies, too," I add. All I remember of my short stint as a Brownie was playing ladder, where girls lay down like rungs while a Brownie jumped over them. When it was my turn, I was afraid of crushing someone's fingers. And when I was a rung, I lay with my nose plastered against the dusty floor, pressing my arms tightly to my sides, afraid someone would crush me. My uniform was all brown with a shiny brass buckle and an orange kerchief tied tight around my neck. My mother showed me off to my father at the door before I left for my first meeting, spinning me around slowly under her hand.

"Great, now all she needs is a gun," my father said. My mother was furious. She hated it when he talked about guns and bombs and things like that. My father grew up in Germany, during World War II. He was six when it started and twelve when it ended. But my mother grew up here, in Canada.

Danny's about to dip under the hood again. I have an urge to invite him inside. Nobody ever enters this house on my account. Few people, apart from me and my father, and his friend Yurek, enter it at all these days. That's because six months ago, a few days into the new year, my mother split. She left no clue to where she was going, just a note addressed to me that said she'd be in touch soon. I've kept the note, and from time to time I look at it, trying to see if there's some secret message hidden between the words that might tell me where she's gone, but I can't find any. She did sign the note "Love, Mom." I try to tell myself that must mean something, but it's not always easy to believe.

I gather my nerve and call out, "Wanna come in for a drink?"

Danny peeps up from under the hood. "Okay." I stand aside to let him past into the shed. His arm brushes my skin.

"I haven't been in your shed for ages," Danny says, wiping his greasy hands on his jeans.

"Guess not," I respond, looking up behind him to the rafters where my eyes catch sight of the wagon that my father made for me when I was a kid.

"Hey, Danny. Do you remember that wagon you used to push me in?" I ask, pointing up to it.

Danny shrugs, "I guess so. Why?"

"Never mind," I respond, waving the wagon away. I mean, what's the point of reminding him how he used to push me around and yell, "Hitler, Hitler, your dad's Hitler." Besides, he wasn't the only one to do it. A lot of the kids on the block used to roll their *r*'s and gurgle to mimic my father's German accent.

Danny and I sit at the kitchen table with the fake marble top. Danny's looking around the room as if he's studying it.

"Looks just like our kitchen," he says finally.

"Ya, they're all the same. Want a drink?"

"Sure." I pour him some grape juice.

"Your dad still make wine?" Danny asks.

"Ya. It's just about the only thing he still does." I didn't know Danny knew about the wine-making. I never tell anyone, probably because it was something my mother disliked so much. She always said it just made him drink more. Danny's still scanning the kitchen, as if he's looking for something specific. He's probably looking for some sign of my mother, to see if it's true that she left. I'm sure the gossip has made its way around the block. The flats which make up our triplexes are stacked one on top of the other and side by side, like tins on a shelf. There's no way to keep secrets around here.

I wouldn't mind finding a clue or two myself, something to help me make sense of her leaving, but the only thing that reminds me of her in this kitchen are the dye spots in the porcelain sink. When I was little, my mother's friend Margie often came over to help her dye her hair. It was my job to catch the drips. Margie told me that if I missed, my mother would go blind. I sat on the edge of the washing machine watching the purplish liquid slide down until it almost hit her eye, then I jumped down to wipe it away, pulling the

11

wet cloth from temple to temple. Once, Margie dyed the hair green by mistake. My mother was terrified that Margie wouldn't be able to fix it before my father came home, but she did. She just laughed her deep laugh — I could see the gum shaking on her tongue — and started the long process all over again.

"I guess you heard about my mother," I say, finally. Danny nods.

"You must miss her," he remarks, looking down at the floor. I just shrug. Last night I overheard Yurek tell my father that it's dangerous for a girl my age to be without a mother. It made me think of a dream I once had where I was chasing my mother on top of a hill that was covered in train tracks. She was running way ahead and laughing, her flaming red hair streaming behind her.

"What are you doing with your life these days?" I ask Danny, mainly to change the subject.

"Not much. Just hanging out. What about you? You finished school yet?"

"Soon," I answer. "In a couple of weeks. I have two more exams, history and math. Then I'm done."

"Going to your grad?" he asks. I shrug.

"The dance is in two weeks, but I haven't decided."

"I'll take you, if you want," Danny says suddenly. "I'll wear my army gear. I got some at the army surplus store — helmet and all."

I chuckle, but don't know what to say. Part of me thinks it would be really neat to show up with

Danny, especially if he wore his army gear. But I have nothing suitable to wear. I did have a graduation dress, but it got ruined only minutes after I tried it on last Christmas. It was a gift, from my mother. It's puzzling, really, why she would think ahead to my graduation and buy me a dress if she knew she'd be leaving, unless she didn't know she'd be leaving when she bought it.

"Nah," I say finally. "Grad dances are stupid anyway. I don't really want to go."

"We could do something else instead," Danny says. "If you want to …"

I'm about to answer when the front door slams shut way at the other end of the flat. I hold my breath. My father enters the kitchen and looks from Danny to me, several times. The way he repeats his actions tells me he's been drinking.

"You remember Danny? He just came in for a drink." My father kind of grunts. "He was just leaving," I add quickly, hoping Danny will take his cue.

"Well, I better get back to work," he says, nodding in a way that says he's understood. He downs his grape juice in one gulp, wipes his mouth on the back of his hand, then his hand on his jeans.

At the shed door he turns around and, making sure my father isn't looking, winks at me.

I notice, as if for the first time, the deep blue of Danny's eyes and the sandy blondness of his curly hair.

Chapter 2

"What the hell was he doing here?" my father asks, pulling open the fridge door a little too forcefully. All he'll find inside are leftovers and rotting food. I haven't done the shopping in ages.

"Nothing," I respond.

My father then gives me a suspicious look that makes me want to scream. I stamp down the hallway to the bathroom, locking the door behind me, and sit on the pink fluffy toilet seat cover, my head in my hands. Unbelievable. I can't have a friend over, and yet his friend Yurek practically lives here now. And I never say anything, in spite of the fact that he gives me the creeps. He's only twenty-two, not that much older than me, and he's way over six feet tall, but he can sneak up on you like a cat. He's forever scaring me, appearing from behind a door when I thought the room was empty, or rising from a chair that I was just planning to sit in. I try to block out my anger by thinking of Danny and the way the sleeves of his T-shirt cut into his muscles.

In front of the medicine cabinet mirror I study my face. I really am starting to look like my mother. We both have dark brown hair, which we've always worn long and parted in the middle, no bangs. Our hazel eyes are the colour of caterpillars, green flecked with brown. It's incredible to think that I'm just one year younger than she was when she married my father. Nobody gets married at eighteen anymore. My father was twenty-five. He'd just immigrated to Canada, a few years earlier, all on his own. My mother told me that my grandmother never trusted my father, probably because of his German accent. They met in 1957, just a dozen years after the war had ended. It didn't help that my mother's father had been killed in the war. He was a pilot and he was shot down somewhere over France, leaving my grandmother a widow with a young girl. My grandmother would prop pillows between my parents on the sofa when my father came to visit, as though she was building some kind of strategic blockade.

A long time ago, my mother used to stand in this same spot, drawing a black beauty mark on her temple. To me, she was already beautiful. I wonder if Danny thinks I'm beautiful.

The tap below me in the small white sink is dripping at a steady pace. It's been leaking like this for ages. Long ago, way before my mother left, my father would've pulled out his tools and fixed it immediately. But not anymore. The place is full of little defects that need mending.

Suddenly, my father starts banging on the door, pulling the handle so hard the eye of the hook is about to fall off. "All right, all right, I'm coming!" I yell through the door. It's impossible to get any privacy in this place.

"What the hell are you doing in there?"

"Nothing," I respond, as if it's any of his business.

While my father is in the bathroom I steal one of his cigarettes from a pack lying on the kitchen table. He'll never notice. At any given time there'll be ten half-smoked packs lying around the flat. Every time I slip a cigarette out of the silver lining I feel as though I'm getting back at my father for not doing more to find my mother. It's as though he hasn't really noticed that she's gone yet. He never mentions her in any way. When Yurek does, he just looks away, or keeps drinking his wine as if he hasn't heard, or as if he doesn't care.

Once, when he thought my father wasn't listening, Yurek pulled me aside.

"You should have more compassion," he said. "It isn't easy for a man to lose his wife."

I wanted to laugh. Yurek is my father's only friend left from the bottle factory, which is where my father used to work until he got fired a year and a half ago. Yurek comes over and yells, "I am fighting for you, my friend." He was some kind of revolutionary in Poland before he left, or got out, as he puts it. I think he's happy to have someone to fight for again. He's only been in Canada for two years and has been sticking to my father like glue ever since. Maybe he sees my father as some sort of father-figure. I should tell him that he's made a lousy choice, but it wouldn't do any good. He's completely loyal to my father, always trying to explain him to me. But what does he know about my parents' relationship? I'm sure he only has my father's version to go by. He doesn't know what bothered my mother. Like the way my father lost his job and the fact that he was always home after that. She said she felt like her space had been invaded, as though my father were an alien. And she hated his drinking. That's why she wouldn't go near his wine cellar. My father used to call her over. "Come see, there's nothing to it." But she wouldn't look. Whenever he was down there, I wasn't allowed in the shed because he had to keep the top up, for air. "She'll fall right in and break her neck," my mother would say. Sometimes, when my mother wasn't around, I'd peek in. My father's arms would reach up to me and he'd whisper "I'll hold you, I'll hold you." But at the last minute I always got scared and ran away.

I head out through the shed. Danny's still fiddling around with a mass of wires and engine parts that mean absolutely nothing to me. "Wanna come have a smoke?" I ask.

"Sure, give me a minute." Danny collects his

tools inside a gray canvas bag and then locks them into the car. He shuts the radio off halfway through my favourite Fleetwood Mac song. We head down the lane, past the backs of the brick triplexes with their tin sheds and rickety wooden stairs.

"Wanna go to the French schoolyard?" I ask. It's where lots of teenagers hang out. People bring ghetto blasters and beer or whatever. I never go myself, but I often see the mess they leave behind. The cement is littered with smashed bottles and cigarette butts. The walls of the school have been totally covered in fleurs-de-lys, the symbol of Quebec, and slogans like "Vive le Quebec libre." I was only ten when the FLQ, a terrorist group in Quebec, kidnapped two important men, killed one of them, and sent the rest of the province into mass panic. The army was even called in to patrol the streets. I remember going downtown with my mother and seeing soldiers with rifles pacing up and down. It made my mother nervous and she squeezed my hand so tightly I thought she'd crush my bones.

"No. I hate that schoolyard. I'll show you my own secret hideaway. Come on." Danny takes my hand and we run all the way to the top of the lane, to the back of the Catholic church.

"Come on," Danny says, pulling me down a deep narrow staircase that leads to a closed door.

"Where does that door lead to?" I ask.

"To the dungeon. Where they keep all the old

18

statues and dead priests," Danny says. He says everything with such a straight face that I can't tell when he's joking. "Just kidding. It's the basement." He pulls the handle, as though by some miracle the door will open. Of course, it's locked.

"Wouldn't the priest be there?" I ask

"Nah. Priests don't work during the week." The landing we're standing on is only big enough to hold a steel garbage can. We settle onto the concrete stairs and light our cigarettes. Danny can blow perfect smoke rings.

"Did you learn that in the army?" I ask him.

"Sure. Watch." The smoke rings rise into the air, then lose shape.

I don't like being this deep down. It reminds me of my father's wine cellar and of the hole in his old house in Germany, which I visited when I was twelve. It was in the root cellar, buried under a heap of potatoes. He said they had dug it out in case someone had to hide. He pulled the trap door up to show me, and the pungent smell of moldy earth hit my face. I remember thinking that I'd die if I had to hide down there. "Doesn't this place give you the creeps?" I ask.

"No. Why? I like it down here." I wonder if Danny misses his father as much as I miss my mother. But I don't dare ask. When we were kids, Danny's father used to work in his brother's furniture store around the corner, until he disappeared. Danny told everyone that his dad was in Africa, preaching to the poor, like some missionary. Wherever he went, he never returned, and Danny never mentions him.

"Are you going to look for your mother, Sandra?" Danny asks finally. The question is so blunt it shocks me. Of course, I want to find her. I just don't know where to begin, or how. Besides, up until now, I guess I believed she would get in touch, like her note said.

"I'd like to, but I don't really know how," I admit.

"We could take my car, you know," Danny offers.

"Thanks, but I wouldn't know where to go. I mean, it's a big city. She's probably got her own apartment somewhere, but how do we figure out where?" I can picture my mother in her own small apartment. She somehow always seemed alone. She even looks alone in the wedding picture that's still sitting in its gold frame on our bookshelf. In it, she's leaning back on my grandmother's threadbare sofa, a full foot away from my father. The few wedding guests are just blurs in the background, sitting on the fold-out chairs from the kitchen.

We grind our cigarettes out on the concrete with the heels of our running shoes.

"Well, I better go," I say. "I have to start supper." I pop some gum into my mouth to cover up the smell of smoke on my breath, a futile gesture since no one comes close enough to notice. When we emerge from the stairwell, the late afternoon sun is blinding.

When we reach his backyard, Danny says, "Maybe we could go for a drive tonight?"

"Okay. But don't ring the bell. Just knock lightly on the back door."

Danny nods and waves goodbye.

When I open the back door, I can hear Yurek's voice beyond the shed, in the kitchen, ranting about some work issue. I suppose this means he'll stay for supper. It happens without any kind of formal invitation, and I can't seem to find a way of stopping it. It's like an unstated agreement, one of many in our house.

I take a deep breath and enter.

Chapter 3

Now that my mother's gone, I'm the family cook. Somehow, the job has just fallen onto my shoulders. I guess it was either that or starve. I've never seen my father make anything more complicated than toast. Not that I have much cooking experience myself, apart from Home Ec. classes at school, where we learned to make meat sauce and pineapple chicken. I do remember some of the dishes my mother used to make because I always did my homework at the kitchen table, often while she was preparing supper.

Tonight, I decide to be extravagant and make lasagna. I make it just the way I remember my mother making it, layering the noodles, sauce, and cheese delicately and precisely, like a bricklayer. My father is in good spirits, and Yurek has been talking about getting him back into the factory.

"We have petition," he says. He pulls the paper out of his shirt pocket, unfolds it, and dangles it in front of my face, then my father's. My father's eyes scan the names with a concentration that is rare for him these days. I picture him filling the lunch table at the bottle factory with the people whose names appear on the list. My father packed the same lunch every day for seventeen years — a salami sandwich and an apple. Every so often, my mother tried to talk him into buying his lunch for a change. But he always said that he'd rather die than eat their food, as though the factory was his enemy and he was a prisoner of war. He even used to push the free tea and biscuit aside at break.

"We get you back in," Yurek promises, smiling wide. He has black holes in his teeth, probably from his diet back in Poland where he was very poor. "We have union."

Yurek says this to me, with a wink. The word enrages my father and Yurek knows this. He hates unions because he doesn't trust organized groups of any kind. Also, the union didn't do much to support him when he got fired.

I clean up to the sound of Yurek's plotting voice. I want to scream that all the petitions, unions, and tactics in the world won't get a man who refuses to follow orders his job back. That's why he lost his job in the first place, because he exploded the day his boss announced that the plant was becoming automated and that all the mechanics, my father included, would need to take some courses. After that, each mechanic would be in charge of a given number of machines, in a single section of the factory. My father saw this as restrictive, undemocratic even. He was used to hearing his name over the intercom, summoning him to the next trouble spot. The boss tried to convince him this would give him more authority, not less. He could be king of his own little bottle-machine empire. But my father didn't buy it. He can't stand feeling that he's being forced to do something, or worse, being fenced in in any way. Yurek once told me that my father had to participate in the Hitler Youth. There, the kids had to stage mock battles in the woods and capture each other's flags. One day, he stole the German flag, just for a joke, and buried it in the snow. My father apparently got beaten across the palms with a stick for that, and the experience made him almost allergic to authority of any kind. Anyway, my father took his protests at the factory a little too far. He'd saunter from job to job, taking ten times longer than he should have. He once left a wrench inside a machine, which wrecked it. Then, when management caught him trying to talk other mechanics into doing similar things, they sacked him, just like that, after fifteen years of service.

Danny knocks lightly, as I told him to. I tiptoe to the back door.

"Wait here for a few minutes. I'll be back."

My father and Yurek have settled into their spots in the living room. The news is blaring and their eyes are glued to the television screen, but I doubt they're listening. My father has gone to that faraway place only he inhabits, and Yurek is probably back on the warpath, scheming in his mind. It isn't hard for me to grab my jean jacket and walk by without attracting any attention.

"See you later," I call from the kitchen. No one answers.

I settle into Danny's car, a battered Monte Carlo with a long hood and short trunk. A "disco sucks" sticker is now decorating the bumper. We're at the end of the lane when I think of it.

"Stop. Let's get Siberia."

Danny slams on the brakes and shifts into reverse. We back up all the way to the yard next door to my house. Siberia is old now; she doesn't jump up when I approach the gate like she used to. She's resigned to her captivity. I ease my fingers through the bars and untwist the metal knot that secures the gate, keeping one eye on the back door. Siberia's owner used to throw buckets of hot water on us when we'd try to pet the dog and people gave up calling the Humane Society to report his cruelty years ago. The dog was at least fed, never beaten, end of story for them. But I can't remember ever seeing her outside this two by four cage-like yard.

"Come on, Siberia," I coax, making kissing sounds and rubbing my fingers together. Years ago she would have come running. Now, she looks up at me with wet eyes.

"She doesn't want to come, Sandra," Danny calls from the car.

"Yes, she does, just gimme a minute." I loop a

finger into her collar and pull gently. She comes, slow and hazy, like a drugged patient. I retwist the wire then push Siberia gently onto the back seat. I have no idea where we're going and I don't care, either. Danny seems to know his way around and that's good enough for me. It feels great just to be leaving the neighbourhood.

"Ever been this way before?" Danny asks.

"I don't think so."

"We're going to Kanawake." Of course I've heard of it. In school, whenever we talked about Canadian history, the teachers would remind us that there was an Indian reserve just across the river, as if that made us special.

"Why?" I ask.

"To get some smokes. They're real cheap there."

We travel south on a maze of concrete ribbons, finally hitting the Mercier bridge. As we cross it, I stare out the back window at the Montreal skyline, the tall buildings hugging Mount Royal like the peaks of a crown. Siberia is curled up on the back seat. I dig my fingers into her fur and scratch her chin. Her watery eyes look up at me, as if to tell me she's okay. Below us, the St. Lawrence river is rushing angrily toward the Atlantic Ocean. A few kilometres past the bridge, Danny pulls up to a shack with a wooden "cigarette" sign over the front. An old woman is sitting outside on a stool. She doesn't look up as we pass, but when she sees Siberia she holds out two fingers for the dog to sniff. Siberia goes to her and the woman runs her dark fingers through the long, white fur.

Inside, Danny orders a carton from the woman behind the counter. She disappears through a curtained door and comes back with it. She takes Danny's money and puts it into an old cigar box. We thank her and she nods.

Outside, Siberia has sprawled herself out at the feet of the old woman, curled around her legs like large furry slippers. I stand a few feet back and call the dog's name, but she doesn't budge.

"She doesn't want to go," the old woman announces flatly, staring down at Siberia.

"Maybe she doesn't like cars," I respond awkwardly.

Danny is getting kind of impatient, gunning the engine. I look over to him and raise my shoulders. The woman might help by pushing Siberia with her feet, but I can't think of a way of asking her to do this.

"Come on, Siberia," I try one last time, lamely. My smacks of the lip are becoming embarrassing. A smirk is beginning to form around the old woman's mouth.

"Fine then, stay!" I say, and turn to the car. I half hope she'll follow, like a child finally understanding it will be stranded, but she doesn't.

As Danny backs out, the wheels spit up dust and gravel. Through the cloud, I watch Siberia lift her head lazily while the Indian woman scratches her furry chin, the two of them turning their backs on us as though we never existed.

Chapter 4

Yurek has taken a map of Montreal and drawn Xs over all the possible places my mother could have gone.

"In Poland we always find people through people," Yurek explains. He has spent every night this week getting as much information about my mother as possible out of my father. He has had to make several trips to the wine cellar to do this, because my father only talks about her when he's had far too much to drink. Right now, even though it's three o'clock on a Saturday, he's still sleeping this one off.

"Yurek, you're crazy, you know that?"

"Why crazy? Your mother should be here with you, with your father."

I shrug and ask him to show me his map.

"Maybe with this aunt," Yurek says.

It's an X over in the east end at my great aunt's place. I only met her once, when I was really little.

She lived with forty cats in a small flat. I had to hold my nose it smelled so bad, and it scared me to watch the way the cats walked along the stove where the water for tea had just boiled, gingerly curling their tails away from the heat.

"My mother wouldn't go there, Yurek, I'm sure of it. That aunt must be dead by now. And she has no other relatives, none that she'd want to find, anyway."

Yurek wrinkles his bushy brow. He can't understand the way we live, all split up. I contemplate telling him how my mother cut herself off from her family, even though it was a small one, when she married my father.

There's an *X* down near the canal, in a part of the city I've never been to.

"Who lives there?" I ask.

"I don't know, but your father he points again and again to this place."

Another *X* is right across the street, at Margie's, my mother's old friend. Now I understand why Yurek often stares up at her third floor balcony. He's looking for my mother, hoping to see her wander onto the stage like Juliet.

"Yurek, you are joking, right?" He tells me he isn't and that it happened once in Warsaw to a friend of his whose wife ran away and the whole time was living just down the hall, in another apartment.

"How did she go out? What did she do? " I ask. Yurek shrugs.

I don't like the thought of my mother just across the street. Of course, that was the first place I went when I came home from school to discover she was gone. I was sure Margie would know something, not because they'd been all that close lately, but because I was sure my mother would need help. She had never organized anything, except grocery shopping, and that was easy because the store delivered. We hadn't been on a family holiday since our trip to Germany, and my father had organized that. I remember the way he came home one Saturday waving the plane tickets and announced that we were going. My mother was as surprised as I was, which makes me think he hadn't consulted her beforehand. How then could she organize a getaway?

Then there's an X downtown that could signify a number of places — a restaurant, bar, hotel, or store.

"What do you think we should do? Patrol around downtown night and day?"

Yurek looks dejected. He probably thought I'd throw my arms around him and reward his efforts with a big kiss.

"Thanks for trying, Yurek, but it's no use. One day she'll call or come back."

I say this, but I have trouble believing it myself. I'm beginning to feel like my mother is nowhere. She's been zapped away, sucked up into the lens of some machine, the way an old television screen turns to dots that spin and spin to a small point of light in the centre. My hopes of her getting in touch, like she said she would six months ago, are fading.

Yurek hands me the map and leaves. In the privacy of my own room, I take a closer look at it. In a way it bothers me that Yurek was the one to draw it, even though I don't believe the *X*s mean a thing. It should've been me or my father devising a plan, even a pitiful one like this. What if my mother somehow knows we haven't, and that's why she hasn't called. What if she's testing us? If she is, we're definitely failing her test.

Maybe, with Danny's help, I can start to pass it. After all, he did offer to drive me around to look for her. But it'll have to wait a while. He's gone to Cornwall to visit his cousin who owns a garage. We only went out together once, the night we kidnapped, or dognapped, Siberia, but I kind of miss him. There isn't much to do around here, except sit around and worry about whether or not I passed my exams. I think I did okay. At least I felt pretty good when I was writing them last week.

Not that anyone around here seems to care. I don't even think my father's aware that this is my last year of high school. I could be going into Grade 8 for all he knows. He hasn't asked me what I plan to do next year. Not that I'd be able to answer that question. I don't have a single clue myself. The deadline to apply to college was in March, but I just couldn't be bothered, which means that door is completely shut to me. My only other options are to work or do nothing.

Some choice!

Chapter 5

On my way out to meet Danny the following Saturday night, I discover that the man next door has plastered his fence with signs that read:

Lost One Husky
Long White Fur
Reward

He has put up so many flyers that it's almost impossible to see into the yard. I feel a slight pang of guilt, but I console myself with the thought that Siberia's probably happier where she is.

"Serves him right, the bloody fool," my father says. "Thinks all he has to do is put up a sign?" He stands at the kitchen window for a long time, as if waiting to see whether the signs bring results. A sudden picture of our own back fence comes to me:

Lost One Mother
Long Red Hair
Reward

I think I would add: Answers to the name Anna. I briefly consider sharing this plan with my father, but don't. We never mention my mother, in any way, least of all how to find her.

My father doesn't pay any attention to me walking out the kitchen door and into the shed to leave to meet Danny. I feel I've made a narrow escape. When Danny got back from Cornwall on Wednesday night we went for a drive. I got home kind of late. I didn't even know my father had seen me leave, or realized that I was gone. With my door closed I could've just been in my room. But he was waiting up.

"Where in the hell were you?" he asked the minute I stepped into the kitchen.

"Out."

"Don't get smart with me. I know you were out. Where?"

"Just for a drive."

"A drive. Very fancy," he snickered. And then all of a sudden, "You spend too much time with that Danny. I don't like it. I don't like him. He's a bum, just like his father."

I had to bite my tongue to keep the obvious from spilling out. Wasn't this a great example of the pot calling the kettle black? My father hadn't reacted this way to anything I'd done in a long time. He usually just stays out of my way, especially since my mother left. I couldn't figure out why he was so angry. Does he really care who I go out with? And why did he wait up? Did he think I might not come back?

Whatever the reason, I don't want to go through that again, so Danny and I have developed a secret signal where he honks three times, then I meet him at the empty lot at the corner. If my father has noticed, he doesn't let on. Maybe it's his new job that keeps him distracted. I was the one who got it started.

"Jacques's freezer is out," I told him one day when I came home from the corner store.

"Oh, ya," he said. I took this as a sign of interest.

"Ya. I told him maybe you'd come look at it, for the right price." My father was in his under-shirt and sweat pants, a beer in one hand, a cigarette in the other, the news droning on. I knew not to push.

"He want me to go tonight?"

"If you can."

So he went. It nearly floored me, and as he hauled on his jacket I took back every adjective I had used to describe him lately.

This evening I'm going to meet Danny with Yurek's map tucked in my jeans pocket. It was Danny's idea. When I told him about the map, he said maps and cars go together. I don't tell Danny, but as we start driving, I think about how tonight is the night of the grad dance. Anyway, I'd rather take off with Danny than see anyone from high school. It's as though my former classmates and I are now in separate universes. As they're setting off in fancy dresses, I'm in my oldest jeans and T-shirt, heading to some unknown X in Danny's old car.

It's the X down near the water that we're exploring today. The map takes us under a tangled mess of highway arms that span the southwest part of the city, most of them arching over railroad tracks that are overgrown with weeds. Then we drive through a long, dimly lit tunnel where a sidewalk runs beside us, separated by guardrails. I picture my mother walking along here and I shiver. It looks like it would be rat-infested. It's so dingy and dirty. What would my mother be doing here?

When we emerge into the summer light, we're in the middle of an old neighbourhood full of warehouses and factories. The buildings are old, with painted advertisements of soft drinks I've never heard of faded into the brick. Most of their windows are cracked or broken. Now I really can't understand why my father insisted on this X.

"This is ridiculous, you know. There's nothing here," I say. I'm starting to regret this trip.

"Probably not, Sandra, but this'll be an adventure. Let's keep going and check it out." We end up at the Lachine Canal, and can drive no further. We park behind a closed warehouse and climb the embankment to the path that runs beside the canal. The water is brown and littered with beer bottles and chip bags.

"Let's just walk around a bit and see what we see," Danny suggests.

I follow, keeping my eyes off the water. It's too creepy. Sharp bushes poke through my jeans, as if angered by our intrusion.

"Danny, there's nothing here. Let's go back," I plead. But Danny's pointing ahead to a cluster of abandoned railway cars.

"What the hell do you want to do there?" I ask. But he's gone, climbing up the ladder that hangs down the side of a yellow open-top, swinging his leg over as if he's just climbing the backyard fence at home. His muted voice booms out at me to follow.

When I yell back "no!" Danny sticks his head over the top.

"It's all right, it's perfectly safe. Come on," he urges. I have a sudden flash of my father urging me to come see his wine cellar when I was younger.

I can't really see any way out of it. I'd be too scared to walk back to the car alone. So, I climb wearily, dizzy with the height. After I jump down, I have to squint at first to see. The boxcar is empty, except for odd pieces of unrecognizable clothing, empty bottles, and cigarette butts.

"This is lovely. Now can we go?" I ask sarcastically. I can't believe I'm actually in an old boxcar.

"I don't know what your problem is. I thought you were more adventurous," Danny says, standing with his legs apart and his hands on his hips, like a cowboy in an old Western film. "Come here." He beckons with his finger, and I go to him. We sit down and I lean against his chest. He puts his arm around me.

"Why?" I ask him.

"Why what?"

"Why would my father point to this place?"

Danny holds me back at arm's length and stares into my eyes. "Sandra! He was drunk. He was probably just pointing to the wrong place. His finger was slipping."

I know he's probably right, but still I'm overcome, and for the first time since my mother disappeared, I cry. I bury my face in the hollow between Danny's neck and shoulder, and cry. It's a quiet, noiseless weeping, a steady flow of warm tears that seems unstoppable.

On the way home, I sit close to Danny and he drives with one arm around me. We've never done this before. It feels nice. "Moondance" is blaring on the radio. When we hit our street I reach out and turn the knob on low. I'm really sorry when we pull up to my house.

"I wish we could keep driving forever," I say.

"Ya, me too." Then Danny bends down and kisses me. It feels really sweet. I just hope my father isn't looking out the window.

"See you tomorrow," I say, getting out of the car reluctantly. As I walk up the front stairs I think about how I probably wouldn't have had as good a time at my grad, even if Danny had worn his army gear. I just can't imagine dancing and partying just now. It wouldn't seem right.

I tiptoe through the flat, not wanting to wake my father. But, as I step past his closed door he steps out. His eyes are half-closed and he seems dazed. Before I know it, his hand reaches out and hits my chin and I land beside the sofa.

"Slut," he whispers, then turns back into his room.

Chapter 6

The next morning I wake up to a sore jaw. I stumble over to my bureau and look in the mirror. Sure enough, there's a purple bruise the size of a quarter on the underside of my chin. There's no way I'm going to be able to hide it. I don't wear makeup and it's too hot in July to wear a turtleneck. In the kitchen, I find some money on the fake marble table, on top of a badly scribbled note that says, "grocery money." Ha! It's more like guilt money. I can't believe he thinks he's giving me something to make up for hitting me, when all he really wants is more food in the fridge. Tough. I'm going to take it and spend every penny on myself.

I don't see my father all day. He's obviously hiding somewhere, which is fine by me. I stay in my room listening to music, until I hear Danny honking in the back at about eight o'clock.

"Want to go check out our spot?" Danny asks, winking. Then he notices the bruise on my chin.

"Your father?" he asks. I nod, but he doesn't pry. Danny's not dumb. When he was a kid he often had black eyes. Nobody ever asked why because we knew he'd explode.

I know Danny means the boxcar. Where else? He speeds us there in half an hour this time, now that he knows the way. He has to light a match for me as I descend, because the sun is already setting and the boxcar is dim. I feel like we've entered some abandoned motel and should hang a Do Not Disturb sign on the ladder. We settle into the same corner. Danny's brought some beer along tonight, but it's warm from sitting in his trunk for too long.

"Cheers," he says, clinking my bottle with his.

"What are we toasting?" I ask him.

"Whatever," he says, shrugging. I wonder if Danny ever thinks about what he's going to do with himself once summer's over. I suppose that other kids who graduated are looking forward to college or trying to find jobs. I hear their conversations with their parents in my mind, talking about interests and courses and possible careers. Or perhaps I'm just imagining it all, hearing some script from a rose-tinted TV show, the kind with the perfect nuclear family, like the Brady Bunch or the Waltons. I mean, it's not as though I'm surrounded by doctors and lawyers in my neighbourhood. I can't even think of a single adult on the street who has a university degree. My father has an electrician's certificate from a trade school pinned up to the shed wall with a thumb tack. That's the closest

40

thing to a diploma I've ever seen.

"Do you ever think about what you're gonna do this year, Danny?" He shrugs again. He doesn't know either, even though he's been out of school one year longer than I have.

"I might try the army again. My buddy thinks I should," he says. "You?"

"Get a job, I guess," I respond lamely, not really believing it. I mean, what kind of job could I get? I could be a waitress, I suppose. My typing's pretty good, so I might get an office job. I start to think about what I'd really like to do if the sky was my limit — veterinarian, teacher, nuclear physicist. But the sky isn't my limit. My limit seems to be somewhere lower, like down around the rim of this boxcar.

"Ya sure, a job," Danny says, sarcastically. He snickers, blowing up smoke rings and then poking the nose of his beer bottle through them.

Then, as if the whole conversation has left a bad taste in his mouth, Danny gulps down the rest of his beer. Then he bends down and starts to kiss me. His mouth feels hot on mine. My chin is kind of sore and I want to tell him, but before I know it he's pulling at my T-shirt, lifting it over my head. Then he strips off his own. I run my fingers over his chest, feeling his muscles and the ribs below them. He stops to take off his jeans, then helps me with mine. I've never seen a guy naked before, or been naked in front of one. The half moon beams like a watchful eye above us, letting in just a little

41

light, enough to keep us partly shadowed. I'm glad because the whole thing feels kind of strange. The parts of my skin that touch the metal base are cold. As if Danny knows this, he pulls his jean jacket under me. And then he is on top of me. I let out a gasp, but I don't think he hears it. Our bodies are now one melting mass, our sounds echoing off the steel walls. It feels good, but unbelievable. I almost feel like part of me is sitting on top of the boxcar looking down, watching the whole thing. My first time.

Afterwards, we lie back and stare at the starless sky. The white beam that shines off the top of Place Ville-Marie passes over us once every minute, like some strange pulse from the city's heart.

"What is that light for?" I once asked my father.

"It's a search light," he answered.

"For what?"

"Bomber planes," he said, chuckling. My mother shot him an angry look and stamped into the house.

"You don't have to worry. I pulled out in time," Danny says, snapping me back to the present. "Next time I'll use a condom."

I can't believe Danny's already talking about next time. He seems so sure there will be one. I don't know whether to take that as a compliment or not. I mean, he must like me. But does it mean I gave in too easily as well? How would I know? Who would I ask?

I just nod, to tell him that would be a good idea.

Chapter 7

At supper the next night, Yurek announces that he has made progress in getting my father his job back. The petition has grown and names now cover two sides of the sheet. I picture Yurek leaning over people while they're trying to eat, separating trays to make room for the paper. My father is to go in for an interview tomorrow. Just by coincidence, I have made my father's favourite dish for supper, chicken paprika. It turns out to be Yurek's favourite dish as well. They smack their way through the meal, and when they've finished they both lean back and pat their bellies.

"Your daughter, she is excellent cook," Yurek announces, letting his eyes linger on me for longer than I like. My father notices too, and he reacts by staring straight down at his plate, as though he can block us out that way. I think the word "daughter" embarrasses him. It stresses the connection between us too strongly.

The next morning I'm woken by sounds that belong to the past — the toaster popping, the clink and clank of breakfast dishes. The sun is just starting to rise and the shadows in my room are smoky gray. Then I remember the interview. I feel as though I should do something nice for my father, like iron a shirt or pack him a lunch. Both futile, since his shirts are all permanent press and he won't be staying for lunch. I hear his plate hit the sink. I know a walk down the hall will follow. Then he'll get his jacket from the cupboard and click the front door shut behind him. Even though I haven't heard the routine for two years now, it's etched into my brain, like a record.

When I step out into the hallway, he's just pulling the door closed behind him. He turns back and sees me.

"Good luck," I call out, my voice raspy with sleep.

"Thanks," he responds. He doesn't look at me when he says this, but aims the word somewhere above my head.

When he's gone, I think that maybe I should have smelled his breath and frisked him, or checked his clothes for dangling threads or creases. My mother never fussed over him in the morning, but then she never saw him off to an interview like this. I wonder if she fussed over him the day he had his original interview for the job. I was just a newborn then. I've only seen the bottle factory up close once. My mother took me there to surprise my father with my first report card, in Grade 1. We stood across the street from the big brick building, and when the bell that signalled the end of shift peeled into the air, we were both startled by its loudness. Then the double doors flew open and hundreds of people rushed out into the street. We almost missed my father entirely, he was so buried among the crowd, but eventually he looked across the street and saw us.

My father's plate stares up at me from the sink, a fork and spoon across it like the bones of a poison sign. The single cup beside it seems to accuse me of some sort of negligence. Was I supposed to get up and share a cup of tea with him, offer him some moral support? That'd be a laugh. My father has never even asked to see my high school diploma. It came in the mail last week, because I didn't go to the ceremony. I figured why bother. There'd be nobody in the audience to see me. It's still in the envelope, somewhere on my cupboard floor. Nobody but me knows that I graduated with distinction, for having an overall average in the top ten percent of my graduating class. Not only that, but I've won an award for the second highest mark in math. If I want it, I'll have to go the school to pick it up because it can't be sent in the mail.

I've decided that today is the day I'll begin looking for a job. I can't keep putting it off forever. So, as soon as the corner store opens, I run down to buy a newspaper. Jacques asks me how my father is doing. His freezer, he tells me, has never worked better. My father, it seems, has magic hands where wires are concerned. He tells me he's going to pass my father's name on to all his buddies who own small businesses. "That's nice," I say, trying to sound genuine.

At home, I spread the classified section open on the kitchen table and circle ads that I think I'm right for. Each circle is a new world opening up. I see it all — the bus ride there, the work, the pay-cheque, and at the end of it all my very own apartment. That's when my real life will begin.

Next, I skim down to the personals. It seems that everybody wants somebody, and most of the requirements are the same: Mature, fun-loving, attractive. Some messages are indecipherable. "Wendy thanking Peter for a magical evening." "Dave, please collect your diving gear (wink wink)." "Anna, if you're out there please come home."

Anna, if you're out there please come home.

My eyes travel the sentence slowly, again and again, afraid that if I pull them away the words will vanish.

The ad isn't signed. Presumably, Anna will know who to come home to. How many Annas are missing, I wonder? This ad must have been written for another missing Anna. If I didn't place it, then it couldn't be for my mother. But she might still see it and think that it's for her. Again, I feel a pang of guilt like I did when Yurek gave me his stupid map. My father or I should have placed this ad, or one like it. Hopefully, if my mother sees it, she'll think it was us.

I fold the newspaper and abandon my short-lived job search. I spend the day cleaning up instead. I scrub with furious energy at the many layers of grime that have solidified on the stove-top. I mop both the kitchen and bathroom floors, scrape away bathrings that mark the many months that have passed since my mother's departure, and vacuum up the large dustballs that roam the flat like desert creatures.

My father's red toolbox is sitting on the kitchen counter, its three-tiered shelves opened up on either side. I wonder what it's doing there. Maybe my father was looking at his old tools this morn-ing before going in for his interview, to psyche himself up, to reconnect mentally with the job he used to do. I decide to clean it out. I find some old jars in the shed and sift through the metal to sepa-rate screws from nails and nuts from hooks and other oddly shaped bits and pieces that I don't know the names for. I work on this task for a full hour, filling the jars and reloading the box in per-fect order. When I was very young, before I even started school, I used to accompany my father on his jobs around the neighbourhood. I passed him wrenches and needle-nose pliers, tools other kids my age had never even heard of, pretending that we were doctor and nurse saving the life of some important person, and not merely fixing a refrig-erator. It was fun and I felt really important.

By the time I'm finished, it's twelve o'clock. My father should be home soon, unless he's stopping off somewhere. I wonder if he'll even notice that I've cleaned.

Oh well. Even if he doesn't, I feel better knowing that Anna, if she's out there, will have a clean house to come home to.

Chapter 8

That weekend, when my father is out on a small job, Yurek comes over. He tells me how happy all the men at the factory were to see my father again, how he made the rounds after his interview, screaming "hello!" over the loud machinery. He hasn't officially heard if he'll be rehired. Yesterday, he snarled some nasty remarks about how they would probably delay so they could toy with him, like a giant corporate cat with a desperate mouse in its teeth. Only my father refuses to play desperate; he doesn't call them, he just waits patiently.

Yurek is, as always, extremely hopeful. "You will see. We will do it," he says to me, with his wide grin.

When I don't jump up and down for joy, Yurek looks confused. Again, he tells me I should have more compassion. I contemplate telling him that if I lack compassion, I got it from my father. He never even thanked me for cleaning out his tool-box, even though he must have noticed.

"You have good life here," Yurek continues. Next thing you know, he'll be telling me that these are the best years of my life. "You have easy life here. You don't have to work too hard, you have many things, many rooms." Yurek must be comparing me to someone who lived through the war or the depression, or to a Third World person, the kind they like to show close-ups of on the news, with flies crawling over their noses. My life isn't a disaster, but that doesn't mean it's perfect.

"And you are not alone." Yurek moves closer to me on the sofa when he says this.

My hand stifles what might have been a laugh or a scream. Yurek sees himself as my family's saviour. He thinks he can put us all back together, if he just finds the right method — says the right things, reveals the right secrets, presses the right buttons. He doesn't seem to realize that we're drifting further apart. Lately, I've been hooking my bedroom door because my father has begun wandering around in the middle of the night. It gives me the creeps listening to him mumble up and down the hallway.

"Your father, he have very hard time in his life," Yurek says.

I want to scream "had!" to him at the top of my lungs. Yurek just won't give up. I don't want to know anything about my father's past life. I have a vague recollection of his house in Germany, where we stayed when I was twelve. I remember the flour-dusted kitchen, the dairy smell of the pantry, and the way my Oma's cross slapped her chest as she rolled dough. When she lit the gas stove the flames burst out from under her cracked hands. And when she laughed, her face broke into a thousand lines. I remember lots of old men without legs or arms hobbling around the cobblestone streets, and old women with bent backs and sacks of flesh hanging under their chins, fingering vegetables at the market. One day, we had a picnic on the banks of the Danube and my father took us into a clearing behind some trees and showed us the exact spot where he and his friends once kept their stash of found objects — shards of weapons and bits and pieces of the uniforms of the dead.

But I can't really connect these pictures with my father. They seem too far away, and they also seem to have nothing to do with me.

"My family in Poland remember well the war. It was terrible. My father always have nightmares," Yurek is still continuing, even though I have opened up the *TV Times* to block him out. I keep thinking that all I want to do today is check the classifieds to see if "Anna, if you're out there please come home" is still in the paper. It has been all week, and each time I see it I am strangely comforted.

But Yurek won't be silenced. He tells me how my father had to take a wheelbarrow and pick potatoes from a neighbouring field during the war. I picture the bombs falling as my father tears the plants out of the ground. In my mind, I see the potatoes, plump and yellow, nestling under the earth inside little green shells, like grenades. After he's finished speaking, Yurek leans back and grins with satisfaction, as though he's just given me an incomparable gift, and as though I'll fall into his arms with gratitude. But all I feel is anger. I have nowhere to put this information, nowhere to store it. Yurek would like to see me run and throw my arms around my father and kiss him the minute he comes in. To automatically run to get him a beer out of the fridge. To speak softly and kindly to him twenty-four hours a day. To forgive him for not lifting a finger to find my mother.

"Yurek, don't ever tell me another story like that again." I stand and glare at him as I say this. As usual, he looks surprised. He obviously thought being a saviour would be easier than this.

"If you want to be my father's friend that's fine. But just leave me out of it," I snap at him as I turn down the hall toward the sanctuary of my room.

Later that evening, I hear the two of them talking in the living room. Before, I never paid attention. I thought they were just gossiping about work. Now, I wonder if my father is filling in more of his history, feeding Yurek more excuses for his behaviour. How could things that happened thirty years ago excuse him for all the things he did to drive my mother away — things like drinking too much, losing his temper too much, and getting fired?

I need to escape their voices. I hope Danny will come and pick me up. The problem is I won't hear his honks from my room. I have to get to the kitchen and that means passing them. But I'll have to do it. I have to get out. I take a deep breath, like I'm about to dive into a pool, and walk past the living room. Then I sit at the kitchen table for what seems like ages until, finally, I hear the three honks. I don't even bother saying goodbye.

Naturally, we return to the boxcar. Our suite. Our hideaway. Our refuge from the world. We make out again, only this time Danny brings a condom. I'm more prepared for it this time. I feel more involved, and my body moves to respond to Danny's in a way that it didn't last time. But there's still part of me that feels more like it's watching than participating. I guess that's normal. Later, we get dressed and lie still, without speaking.

Suddenly, a groan sounds in the corner, and with it, a black shape rises, lifting an old coat. I scream and jump all at once, then climb the ladder so fast my feet keep slipping on the rungs. I practically fly down the other side. Danny follows. From the boxcar muted curses rise like fog.

I am shaking. Danny puts his arms around me. "It was just an old bum," he says. "Relax."

I know, I know, but still I can't stop shaking.

Chapter 9

It takes the factory a whole month to let my father know that he has been given back his old job, on provisional terms. They're going to test him out for three months. If he's late, drunk, or rude to either his boss or any of the other workers, he'll be thrown out. Again. And, if he survives the test, he'll have to go to Ontario for a week in December to get some computer training, like it or not.

"I tell you we do it, man," Yurek says, ecstatic.

"On goddamned probation. Like an ex-convict," my father replies. But I can tell he's pleased. Even as he swears, he grins. As if to prove this point, he pulls aside the kitchen curtains and laughs at the man next door. "That goddamned fool's still looking for his dog."

"Forget it, man, you get your job back."

"Man" is Yurek's latest expression. I find my tolerance for Yurek steadily slipping, and the fact that he's over here for supper five nights a week doesn't help. I no longer eat with them, though. I take my supper into my bedroom. I just can't stand the ritual anymore, my father ignoring me and Yurek paying me too much attention, as if to compensate. Besides, this way, I can just leave by the window, inconspicuously. Danny has started honking in the front.

Tonight Danny and I are going for a drive to the east end, to do another X. It was Danny's idea. He says our mission would be incomplete if we didn't.

"Mission impossible," I tell him. My mother left eight whole months ago; if she hasn't been in touch by now, she never will be. But even though Yurek's map still seems ridiculous, I haven't yet come up with a better plan.

I had to go through my mother's top drawer, where she kept all her papers and junk, to try to find her aunt's address. There was some strange stuff in there, including a short black wig that I don't recall ever seeing my mother wear. Luckily, I found an old letter, written just after I was born, that was still in its original envelope. But her aunt's probably dead. After all, she was even older than my grandmother, who was eighty when she died seven years ago.

The east end is a lot like our neighbourhood, only the houses are taller and narrower, with fancy carved galleries clinging delicately to their fronts. As we drive east along Notre Dame, the high cement tower of the Olympic Stadium rises into the sky, the concrete stadium poised beneath it like the shell of a large beetle. The Olympics were in Montreal two years ago, but we didn't attend any events. Tickets were too expensive, so we just watched the games on TV, as usual.

Danny parks the car and we head up the street, Danny leading. The closer we get to my mother's aunt's house, the heavier my feet grow.

The door is at the top of a single concrete step, spitting distance from the curb. There is nowhere to stand back and get perspective. Danny rings the bell, which is a brass square that you turn, very old-fashioned. I haven't prepared any speech, just in case. Danny rings the bell a second time.

Finally, a young boy with a runny nose opens the door. His T-shirt rides up his stomach and his finger digs inside his belly button.

A woman's voice shouts down the hall. *"Qui est-ce?"* The boy shrugs.

"Let's get the hell out of here," I say finally, pulling on Danny's arm. He's staring past the boy as though he honestly expects to see my mother at the end of the dark hallway. The mother comes out on the stoop and stares after us, blowing smoke and scratching her head as we retreat.

"Satisfied?" I ask. I'm suddenly really tired of this phony search. I know I went along with it, but now it all seems incredibly stupid.

"Sorry. I don't know what you're so mad about," Danny says as we get back into the car. "It was just a bit of fun."

Fun? I can't believe Danny thinks this is fun. I

see now that Yurek's map has been nothing but summer amusement for Danny, a diversion from his own life. It doesn't even occur to him that traipsing around to odd parts of the city in search of my mother wouldn't really be fun for me. This map has turned her into a game, as if she's no longer a real person, but just a cartoon X.

"Where do you want to go?" Danny asks, turning the key in the ignition.

I wish I could say "home," but that word doesn't bring comfort. I shrug. Let him decide. He always does, anyway.

As we drive westward, Danny tells me he's thinking again about moving to Cornwall, to work in his cousin's garage. "I can drive down some weekends," he says, as if I need reassuring. When we get to the boxcar, I make Danny check it out first before I consent to climb into it. He pulls a stick off the ground and pokes around in the corners — tap tap tap, just like a blind man.

"It's okay. It's empty," he calls up.

I'd rather not be here at all, but it's like there's nowhere left in the whole city to go. Danny settles into our usual corner and holds out the arm that I'm supposed to crawl into, but I'm too restless tonight to even think of lying down.

"Give me your lighter," I say.

"What for?"

"Just give it to me."

I pull Yurek's map from my pocket and set fire to it. The flame grows and swallows the island of

Montreal, spitting it away in ashes. I hold it until the last possible second then let it drop.

"You trying to burn your hand off?" Danny asks.

I don't answer. From my other pocket I pull out the letter with the old aunt's address on it. I drop it into the dying flame.

"Anything else you'd like to burn?" Danny asks sarcastically.

Yes. I'd like to go home and take a big green garbage bag and empty all the contents of my mother's junk drawer, along with all her remaining clothes and make one huge bonfire. If she wasn't coming back, why didn't she take all her stuff with her? That way, I wouldn't expect her back. And I'd know that the words on her stupid note were just that — words. Completely meaningless.

"Bring me the coat." I can see it rising like a bear in the night on the back of the old bum.

"No way, Sandra. You're crazy." So, I get the coat myself. Danny doesn't try to stop me. I hold the tip of the sleeve over the flame. It takes a while because the coat is damp, but eventually it catches. The material sizzles and curls. Across from me, Danny's body shimmers.

When it was still legal, my father used to burn the leaves that fell off the maple tree. My mother and I would stand at the livingroom window and watch him throw matches onto the piles. Once, he stood too close to the fire and I started crying. "Stand back, you're scaring her," my mother called through the screen.

"Ach," my father waved my fear away with his hand. "I've stood closer to bombs than this." And then my mother drew the curtains angrily together.

Even though the boxcar has no roof, it doesn't take long until we're shrouded in smoke.

"Let's get out of here." Danny is calling to me from atop the ladder.

We stand on the narrow path above the canal and watch the smoke rise like a weak signal, petering out just above the metal rim.

And then we're back in the car. Danny drives us up Mount Royal. From its lookout, the panorama of city lights stretches way off into the sky, like long strings of Christmas lights. There was a mountain in the middle of my father's hometown too, with an old castle sitting at the top. The spikes of its round tower were half broken off, like chipped teeth. I liked to run round and round the turret, stopping to stare down at the red-roofed houses of the little town. It scared my mother though, and she'd scream at my father to hold me. Funny, I think, how she was always afraid of me falling, into the wine cellar, off the castle, or even from third-floor balconies. I never did fall for real as a child, but I feel as though I'm on a long, slow fall right now. And all because of her, as surely as if she'd pushed me herself.

Danny is trying to pull me over to his side of the seat. But I want to get out of the car. We never move. We're always hiding away in dark spaces.

"Let's climb up to the cross," I say.

"What for?" Danny asks, but I'm already out of the car and heading up the path. He has no choice but to follow. We climb the steep stone stairs. The cross, which is made of hundreds of light bulbs, is shining above us, lighting our way. At the top, I run to the wire fence that encloses the cross and spread myself out against it. I can feel the heat of the bulbs behind me, warming my back. I imagine my face lit up like a giant beacon for all the city below to see.

"Come over!" I call to Danny. He steps forward reluctantly. Danny hates light. I guess that's why he's always pulling me into dark spaces.

"This is nuts. What're we standing here for?" Danny is standing at attention, completely rigid, as if he's back in the army.

"I don't know. Maybe so that people will see us," I respond.

"Like who?" he asks.

"Like my mother … or your father," I add.

It's the first time I've ever mentioned Danny's father out loud. I thought it would please him to know that I do remember him, but it doesn't. He gives his shoulders and head a huge shrug, and stamps off angrily out of the light.

I'm just about to chase after him when I change my mind. Let him go. Let him crawl back into the darkness of the car. I don't want to leave the light yet. I stand against the fence for a few minutes, but then it occurs to me that he might abandon me here, like we did to Siberia. Danny's just about the only ally I have these days. Even if I don't like where he's led me, at least he's led me somewhere. When he goes to Cornwall, I'll have no one.

It's that thought that makes me call out and take off after him down the stone steps of the mountain.

Chapter 10

September — the time of year when school usually starts, along with the daily routine of getting up and dressed and out the door. At least that's been the story of my life for the past twelve years, but not anymore. Summer has ended and landed me absolutely nowhere.

I look out the kitchen window at the ever-present maple tree, which is just beginning to turn yellow. In a few weeks it'll be a brilliant collage of orange and red. From here, it'll look like it's on fire. But soon after that, October winds will turn it into a skeleton of branches that thins out toward the tips, like an old bony hand reaching for the sky.

At least the tree has Mother Nature to guide it. I wish I could say the same. I can't seem to get motivated enough to even think about what I want to do with the rest of my life. I feel as though I'm waiting for something to happen, for some sign to fall into my lap and guide me. My mother's words,

"I'll be in touch soon," still nag at me. Nine months is not my definition of soon. In that time she could have conceived, grown, and delivered me.

Even my father has returned to his old routine. Every morning, his plate and cup stare up at me, reminding me that only I have nowhere to go and no purpose in life.

Danny is at his cousin's in Cornwall. He called to say that he now knows how to change a brake pad. Then he added with a chuckle, "Maybe now I'll know how to work my own brakes a bit better," and I knew he was talking about our nights in the boxcar. Then he waited for me to say something, but I didn't know what to say. I tried to remember the feel of Danny's body against mine, but it was the cold and hardness of the metal floor beneath me that stuck out most in my mind.

I carry my hot tea into my bedroom and slam the door shut behind me, even though no one else is home. Then I sit on my bed and look around. I can't believe how childish this room still looks, with its cuddly kitten posters and the row of stuffed-animals on my bureau. At my age, it should be plastered in posters of rock stars, like Freddy Mercury and Rod Stewart. But there wouldn't be much point changing it now. I hope I'll be out of here soon, so why bother.

I pull up my blind a couple of inches and watch the street come to life. My eyes are drawn to Margie's third floor balcony. That's the one *X* on Yurek's dumb map that we never investigated, even though Danny wanted to. Suddenly, Margie's door opens and she steps out. I haven't actually seen her in ages. Impulsively, I jump off my bed, throw on my jeans and sweatshirt and run out to follow her down the street.

She heads into Jacques's, and a minute later, so do I. I watch her turn down the fruit and vegetable aisle, where she picks up a tomato and squeezes it. Next, she weighs a cabbage in her hand, holding it up like a bowling ball. If she were to launch it down the aisle it would hit me, dead on.

Once, when I was just a kid, my mother sent me here to buy a lettuce and I came home with a cabbage instead. How was I supposed to know? They looked the same. And I didn't want to ask Jacques, who stood with his arms folded across his chest, guarding the cash. I was still embarrassed about the time he had dropped his bag of change right outside the shop. Coins burst from the rolled papers like seed from overripe fruit, scattering on the sidewalk. A bunch of us dove at the money, stuffing our pockets with coins while Jacques beat at us with a broom. I ran home, as fast as I could, my pockets bursting with money.

When I got home and told my parents what had happened, my father seemed almost proud of me. He said that I didn't have to take the money back, but my mother said I did. She said it would be hard for her to shop at Jacques's if I didn't. In the end I kept it, but I wish now I hadn't. I can still see the way she shrugged, turned her back, and walked away, giving up.

Margie's white-blond hair is rolled up in curlers, pink plastic pins sticking out like bug eyes all over her head. She's been rolling her hair up like this for as long as I can remember. I follow her out the door, to where she stops at the foot of her staircase.

"Well, wanna come up?" she asks, turning to me and speaking over the tops of the grocery bags. I don't respond.

"I seen ya follow me. You might as well come in," she says.

I follow Margie up the winding outside staircase to the second floor balcony then up the narrow indoor staircase that leads to her third floor flat. I stand at the kitchen door while she takes her groceries from the bag and puts them away. I'm amazed by how similar Margie's kitchen is to my own across the street. It's not just the layout, but other little things as well, like the dying plant sitting on top of the hot water tank and the can of Raid on top of the fridge.

"Well, come on in, have a seat. I don't bite. Want a coffee or tea or a soft drink?" I shake my head. Margie lights a cigarette. "Smoke?"

She holds it up to me and I shake my head. Smoking in front of Margie would be too much like smoking in front of my mother. I only started after she left. It was just something to try to get away with, but what's the point? My father doesn't care anyway.

"I don't want anything, thanks."

Margie pulls out a chair across from me. We don't look at each other. Instead, we study the brown-and-white tiled floor. It has the same black chips where bits of tile have been kicked loose, exposing the glue.

"Your kitchen's just like ours," I say.

"They're all the same, I guess. I could stumble through any one of these places blindfolded. I've been in most of them too, you know, at one time or another. I've lived on this street all my life. Isn't that disgusting?" Margie throws her head back and laughs and I don't know what to say.

"But what the hell. You gotta live somewhere," she adds. "I did move away once. When I was married. We moved up to Outremont." Then Margie stops talking altogether and just stares into her steaming coffee.

"I didn't know you were married."

"There's lots of things you don't know about me, kid. You can live on top of someone around here all your life and not know anything about them. Ya, I was married, to a security guard. I fell for his uniform. It was always so crisp and clean. Of course, I only found out later that his mother kept it that way. Washed and ironed it every night, and he expected me to do the same. It used to give me the creeps, hanging on our closet door, like some sort of voyeur. I thought it was watching us."

"How long were you married?" I ask.

"Just a couple of years." Then there's another long silence.

"Eventually I moved back here. Did you know I grew up next door to where you live now, on the first floor?"

"Where Siberia lives? I mean lived?" I am excited now by the connections.

"Ya, that's the one. Guess his dog never came back, eh? Don't blame it. It was a crime the way he kept that beautiful dog all cooped up. Your mother ..." and then Margie's voice trails off. I can feel my face burning.

"Sorry," she says a moment later.

"It's okay. I'm just not used to anyone mentioning her. What were you going to say?" I prod her on, anxious for these little tidbits, even if they don't seem relevant to the present.

"Well, nothing, just that your mother used to feel so sad for that dog. She was always saying that she'd like to slip the latch off the gate one night and let it out, but then where would it go?"

"Well, she's gone now. I guess my mother would be happy."

"Damn right she would be."

There is another pause and then I remember that I've left the door to my own flat unlocked. I ran out in such a hurry. My teeth and hair are unbrushed and I suddenly feel scuzzy.

"I guess I should go," I say.

"Hey, I'm sorry, Honey, if I upset you, talking about your mother. Stay for a minute. I'm already late for work, anyway." Margie seems more anxious for me to stay this time. Last time, I never made it past her front door. She just stood in the doorway, insisting over and over again that she had no idea where my mother had gone. I hesitate before sitting back down. Nobody has called me "Honey" in a long time.

"Tell me what you're doing with yourself these days. You must be finished school now, right?"

I nod. Finished and done. It wouldn't occur to Margie that someone could actually go past high school. I'm sure she herself never gave it a second thought.

"Looking for a job?"

"Sort of," I lie. I haven't looked at a newspaper for a while.

"I might be able to fix you up with something at the hotel. It's not great work, but it's better than nothing." Margie hesitates, as though she is about to add something, then stops.

"Do I have to wear a uniform?" I ask.

"Sure, but you save a lot on clothes. I mean, who the hell cares what you wear before or after your shift."

My shift. The word sounds odd. It's a word I can only connect to my father.

"Well, okay. Why not?" I say.

"Great. Meet me at the bus at quarter to seven."

Chapter 11

The next morning I wait until I hear my father leave before I get up. I feel odd depositing my own cup and plate beside my father's in the stark, white sink. I go out the back door, stepping over the square cellar door with its brass ring. When I pass Siberia's yard I shiver. That weird man is staring out of his kitchen window, scratching his naked belly. Some Lost Dog notices still cling tenaciously to his fence, flapping in the September breeze.

Margie is waiting for me at the bus stop. "All set, Sandra?" she asks. We climb aboard the 80 bus, which is practically empty at this hour. The downtown streets are quiet too — storefronts shut, the homeless beginning to stir, the restaurants filling with the breakfast crowd. I follow Margie down de Maisonneuve to where she stops beside a really small wooden door. Above it hangs a faded wooden sign that says Entree Employee Entrance. I picture the two of us having to drink some sort of magic potion before squeezing through it, like Alice in Wonderland. But then Margie pulls the door open and we bend inside. I'm met by a nauseating smell of garbage that becomes stronger with each step I take downwards.

"Don't worry, Honey, you get used to it," Margie calls out in the near dark. At the bottom she turns to me.

"By the way, did I tell you you have to be eighteen to work here, so just say you are, okay? I mean, you're almost there, right?" I nod.

Margie then leads me through a gray brick hallway. Double doors lead off either side to various operations. The laundry, where men and women in white coats and caps stand around huge plastic tubs, the smell of soap and starch bringing a welcome relief from the stench of garbage further back. A canteen, where a round old woman stares out from a cracked wooden frame in the wall, chip bags clipped up the walls on either side of her. And a lunchroom full of non-descript wooden tables and chairs, all of them at odd angles, as though invisible people were communing. I have a hard time believing that I'm in the Sheraton, the same hotel with the fancy front entrance and glittery lobby.

I follow Margie into an office where she introduces me to a woman sitting behind a large desk. On the wall behind her hangs a great panel of keys. Down the left wall are a series of leather belts, each one also holding a key. Margie calls the woman aside and they whisper together for a few minutes. I imagine she's convincing her that, in spite of my lack of experience, I can do the job. The whole time Margie is talking to her, the woman keeps her eyes glued to my face. Even when I blink and look away, I can feel her eyes on me.

Finally, Margie says goodbye and good luck and disappears through a door that leads to the office where she works. She waves at me through the window in the door as she settles in behind her desk. The woman hands me some forms to fill out. The whole time I'm writing, women come in to pick up the leather belts. I study their faces as they pull cards out of a slotted steel case near the door and stick them into the time clock, thinking that I will soon be one of them. It's kind of hard to imagine, they're all so much older than me.

I finish the forms and hand them to the woman. She looks them over quickly, without smiling. Then she sends me down the hall to be fitted. There, an abrupt woman who speaks no English twists and turns me, measuring me with great big calloused hands. Finally, she throws me a blue uniform and points to yet another form that I have to sign.

Outside, an older chambermaid is impatiently waiting. "*Viens, viens vite*," she says, pointing to her watch. It is 7:45 am.

I shadow my trainer, whose name is Valérie, for the entire day. She shows me how to throw new sheets onto stripped mattresses so that they float down and land perfectly without a wrinkle. She teaches me how to tuck properly, and how to encase the pillows with the bedspread so that not an inch of sheet sticks out. Valérie's hands are thin and raw, but for an older woman she's incredibly strong. When she flings a sheet onto a bed her biceps flex under the short sleeves of the uniform. She teaches me the trick of saving the used towels to shine the chrome in the bathroom after it has been scrubbed, and is adamant about removing steam spots from the mirrors. I can tell by the way Valérie approaches the rooms that she's not curious about the people who've slept in the beds, or drawn smiling faces in the shower steam. She tells me that she has worked here for twenty-seven years. I automatically calculate her tasks — about thirty beds per day times three hundred and sixty-five days, minus the three weeks of vacation time that I assume she gets, times twenty-seven years. That means that she's changed around 300,000 beds and scrubbed over 150,000 toilets in her lifetime!

I follow Valérie from room to room the entire day, but she doesn't let me touch a thing. I just watch and take mental notes. Before we leave the room, Valerie runs a pillowcase over the chair I've just vacated, as though I may have left a stain.

That night, when I tell my father that I've found a job at Margie's hotel, he doesn't say much. He just says, "Oh," and then looks down at his plate. He seems almost disappointed. What did he expect me to do? Announce that I've become a brain surgeon?

But Yurek, who's here for supper again, can't resist putting in his own two cents worth. He tries desperately to trump up this trivial connection between me and my father. "You are comrades now," he says. "Brothers."

I want to point out that, technically, my father and I could never be brothers. This should be obvious to Yurek, who's always trying to point out my better feminine qualities to my father, like the way I cook. Yurek is too dumb to see that his remarks only embarrass my father, who never responds to them.

I want to kill him, yet I know there's a disturbing truth to his words. My father and I are both workers. We'll both be spending our days in company-issued uniforms. Does that mean I'm embarking on a similar path to his? Will I too be working at the same job for the next two decades, leaving the house every morning before the sun is up? Oh well, who cares? At least I'll have my own apartment and I won't have to lock my bedroom door or cook for three people anymore.

I'll just have myself to look after.

Chapter 12

After one week of training, I'm finally allowed to set out on my own. Every morning, I let the time-clock kiss my card, then I look my name up on the worksheet to see which floor and section I've been assigned. Then I pick up the leather belt that holds the master key for the eighteen rooms of my run. I change into my maid uniform in the fourth floor locker room, which is also a kind of lounge where most of the maids eat their lunch. Then I collect my cart from the closet on the floor that I'll be working on. I take a few minutes to stock it with supplies — fresh linens and towels, a tub full of cleaning products, a feather duster, and a box full of complements, such as shower caps, mini-soaps, pens, and bar and restaurant brochures that I have to deposit in each room before leaving. I have a list of all the rooms that are check-out rooms and I have to do these first. Before entering a room with my key, I knock three times and call out, "housekeeping." Then I wait a few seconds before letting myself in.

For my first solo week, Valérie checks my rooms at the end of each shift. I have to rescrub several toilets, remake several beds, and re-vacuum several carpets. Each time, Valérie stands over me, arms crossed, muttering, "*mieux, mieux,*" under her breath, sounding like a cat. When I've cleaned to her satisfaction, she lets out a final sharp, "*Bien.*" That's how I know the job is done.

It takes me about twenty minutes to do each room. I start with the beds, then I wash the bathroom. I save the vacuuming for last because it's the job I like the least. The vacuum cleaners are big industrial ones and they're so loud they give me a headache. But that's the only part I don't like. I love everything else about the job. I especially love the fact that I'm totally on my own. There's no one watching me, no one that I have to talk to. I even take my breaks and eat my lunch alone. I'm not supposed to do this, but sometimes I close the door of a check-out room and watch TV while I'm eating. I pretend I've moved out and the room is my new apartment. Not that I'd really want it to be. This is an elegant but old hotel and the furniture is shabby. The bedspreads and curtains rarely match, and the carpets are so thin you feel you're sucking the last bits of fiber up whenever you vacuum.

Sometimes when I'm cleaning, I picture myself putting matching curtain and bedspread sets back together. I try to keep a mental list of rooms that need rematching, memorizing the colour and pattern of the materials in the rooms. Putting the rooms back together wouldn't be hard to do. One of the busboys, who come around twice a day to collect dirty laundry from my bin, might be willing to help. The only problem is that I never speak to them. They try to joke around with me, but I don't know how to respond to their casual teasing. They make me uncomfortable because I'm usually leaning over half-made beds or scrubbing bathtubs when they come round. The older maids love to giggle and flirt with the busboys. Once, a busboy draped himself in a white sheet and lunged like a ghost at the maid whose bin he was clearing out. Then he chased her down the hallway. She was panting with excitement.

I prefer to amuse myself by looking for clues about the clients. But I have to be careful when I do this because it's strictly against hotel policy to touch any belongings, except if I have to move them for cleaning purposes. I have to be sure that I'm not in sight of the open door when I pull open bureau drawers and peek inside. I've discovered that very few people bother using the drawers. They mostly hang what needs to be hung and keep the rest of their goods in their suitcases. If these are already open, and if I'm out of sight of the door, I sometimes poke through them. But if they're closed, I don't dare pull them open. Either way, I haven't really found anything interesting yet, just the usual travel stuff. Sometimes people leave things behind by mistake after they check out. I've found a couple of hairbrushes, some socks and underwear, and even an ivory cross with a silver Jesus glued to it in the nightstand drawer, next to the Bible.

What I like best about being a chambermaid, though, is that my mind goes perfectly blank while I'm cleaning. I simply focus on the mindless, repetitive tasks. I can almost feel my body taking over and cleaning on automatic pilot. After a while, my mind is free to wander. I mostly think about the two paycheques that I've received so far and the bank account I've opened. I'm going to try to save every penny, and then when I have enough for a couple of months' rent, I'm going to tell my father I'm leaving.

I even really enjoy the early morning bus ride to work. Although we've never officially arranged to do so, Margie and I meet at the bus stop at 6:45 every morning. I like turning the corner to see her there, as if she's somehow there for me, which is silly because she'd be going to work anyway. We don't talk much on the ride downtown. Margie likes to look out the window. Sometimes, she dozes off, her head bumping against the glass. I'm content to sit beside her, counting off the landmarks that line the route. One of them is the gray-stone YMCA on the corner of Park Avenue and Saint-Viateur, where my mother took me for ballet lessons Saturday mornings when I was little.

"Your mother really enjoyed taking you there,

you know?" Margie says to me one morning, as the bus speeds through Outremont. "She liked this part of town. She said it had flavour."

"Do you think she lives here now?" I ask, shyly almost, as if I've broken a rule.

But Margie's head is turned back to the window and her eyes are closed.

I try to imagine what an apartment of my mother's might look like. She used to like to paint things on the walls; long ago there was a tree in the hallway, a sun over my bed, a cat in the bathroom. Perhaps, wherever she is, she's taken her designs one step further. I picture her standing against a wall mural of tall jungle trees, twisting vines, and exotic wildlife, like tigers and zebras.

I make a mental note to myself — Outremont: possible place my mother has gone because she liked it. Her one and only job had been in this area too. It was an after-school and weekend job that she had when she met my father, at Herzel's Leather Shop. He sold shoes, handbags, purses, and belts; anything leather. She once told me that Mr. Herzel's son, Aaron, was always hitting on her. He'd wait on the balcony of the upstairs flat where the family lived and call down to her and wink when she showed up for work. Sometimes he'd hook his finger and motion for her to come up, but she never did. She told me that once he followed her into the supply room and pulled her behind a stack of empty boxes and kissed her — it was her very first kiss.

I don't know if my father knows the story, but if he did I bet that old store would have transformed in to an *X* on Yurek's stupid map. And then Danny would have insisted we check it out. I haven't heard from Danny in a while. I wonder what part of the car he's into now. Has he graduated from the brakes to the engine? Does he like his new job as much as I like mine?

Chapter 13

One morning, in my fourth week on the job, I discover that my daily run contains a suite. I'm really excited because I haven't been inside one yet. They're normally given to the more experienced maids. I save it for mid-morning, to coincide with my break. I intend to linger and luxuriate in it for as long as I can. As I approach the suite, two men step out the door and stop to look me up and down. I try to block them out by busying myself with sorting out my cart.

"It's all yours, babe. Hope we didn't make too much of a mess," one of them says, leaning against my cart. He hasn't shaved yet and the stubble on his chin looks like dirt.

Then both the men laugh and the one who spoke reaches out as if to grab the strings that hold my goofy apron in place. I step back, out of his reach.

"Ooo, playing hard to get?" he says, laughing. I can feel my face turn red. I'm trying to think of something to say, when the other man pulls his friend by the arm and they head off down the hall. One of them lets out a loud belch. I brace myself for what I'll find inside.

I knock loudly, and wait the customary fifteen seconds before peeking my head in and shouting "housekeeping." No one answers, so I enter the suite. There was obviously a party here the night before. The air reeks of alcohol and tobacco. The gold brocade sofa has been practically dismantled, its cushions in a heap on the floor. In the corners of the living room are china cabinets with porcelain sculptures inside. Luckily, these seem to be intact. I stroll around, collecting cigarettes in my apron pocket from the open packs lying around. I tidy up a bit, then pull my cart inside, close the door, and smoke a cigarette sprawled out on top of the reassembled sofa. It's easier to pretend that this is my new apartment because it feels like one, except I doubt mine will have a chandelier. I've just lit my second cigarette when I hear footsteps approaching from the bedroom behind me. I hadn't even thought to check if anyone was in it. I turn around quickly to face a tall, blond woman draped in a sheet, her face still puffy from sleep, her skin blotchy from the makeup she didn't remove the night before.

"What time is it?" she asks.

"Almost ten," I reply, standing up quickly.

"Creeps. Got a smoke?" I point to the pile on the table beside me.

"Sit down, I won't report you," the woman says, waving her polished nails at me. Then she takes a cigarette and disappears into the bathroom and turns on the shower.

I move my cart back outside and occupy myself with vacuuming the plush carpet. The woman emerges a few minutes later, wearing a black leather mini-skirt partially covered by a long gold sweater. Her hair is puffed up like Farah Fawcett's. She motions for me to turn off the machine.

"Hey, is there any way of getting out of this hotel without having to go through the lobby downstairs? You know, a back door or something?"

My mind races to the gray basement and the tiny door. "There is, but it's for employees only." I hesitate, then add, "But I can take you there, I guess." I don't know why I said this. What do I care if she needs to sneak out?

"I'd really appreciate that, kid," she says, smiling. The way she says "kid" makes me feel funny. I tell her to stay put while I check that no other employee is waiting for the back elevator. When it comes, I open the doors, then run to usher her into the hidden hallway. She still looks washed out, in spite of a new layer of makeup.

"I'd hold my breath if I were you," I warn her.

I think ahead to the basement, and of all the movies I've seen where people steal lab coats to sneak out of hospitals. I picture dressing the woman in one of the white coats and caps of the laundry workers, but I've no way of getting hold of any. When we reach the basement, I figure the best thing to do is just walk calmly and try to look as though we're carrying on a casual conversation. At the foot of the back stairway, I step aside and just point up into the dark. In the late afternoons, a security guard stands right here while the maids file past, holding our handbags under his nose for inspection. He's not allowed to touch anything, and I've learned that pens and soap can easily be concealed beneath envelopes or gloves.

My father, when he heard me tell Yurek about this ritual, said he'd never bloody well agree to it. And he went on to tell Yurek how, when he was twelve, he had watched his mother prevent the French soldiers from opening her bureau drawers by standing in front of them, leaning her broad body into the heavy wood. "She could have been killed for that," my father added.

"Watch your head, it's low," I call out to the woman behind me.

"Thanks a lot, kid," she says. And then she pulls a twenty dollar bill from her handbag, hands it to me, and disappears up the dark staircase.

I've almost forgotten where I am as I walk along the gray hall fingering the money.

"Mademoiselle?" I turn to see the woman who first hired me leaning against her office door. She motions for me to step inside. The immense wall of keys behind her catches my eyes. That day, the keys meant nothing, but now I can see that they are individual keys for each and every room in the hotel.

"Mademoiselle, this part of the hotel is for employees only. I saw you take a woman outside?" She raises her pencil-thin eyebrows as she speaks. I can't think of anything to say. How did she see me?

"Why did you bring a woman down here?" Her voice is completely serious, as though I've been caught leaking important documents to foreign agents.

"She was sick. She was in the employee elevator. I didn't know what else to do," I reply, impressed by my quick thinking.

"Hmmm. Well, next time, you can lead her to the clients' elevator. We try not to advertise this entrance. It's not for the public." She stares at me intently for a minute, then dismisses me with her hand.

That afternoon, on the bus ride home, Margie mentions the woman to me as well.

"Running an underground railroad, are you now?" she asks. I think she may be joking, but when I look at her face I can tell that she's serious. I can't believe that my little adventure was so significant. Surely a non-employee has made their way down to the belly of the hotel before now, even if just by mistake. I have a sudden recollection of the dark tunnels below the castle in my father's hometown. I wanted to crawl inside them, but my mother kept screaming at my father to hold me back.

"You've got to be careful not to break any hotel rules, or they'll let you go, Sandra," Margie continues. "They're pretty strict about things."

"Sorry."

"It's okay, but just be careful. You know, she wasn't too keen to take you on. I really had to talk her into it. If you screw up she'll be mad at me too."

I want to ask her why the woman, whose name I still don't know, was so reluctant to hire me, but Margie's eyes are already shut.

Something about the way she turned off so fast makes me think there's something she's not telling me. But what?

Chapter 14

After six weeks on the job, I stop noticing mismatched bedspreads and curtains. There are simply too many rooms at the twelve-storey hotel. The probability of my even repeating the same run twice is very low, unless I were to stay here for the rest of my life. So, to keep myself occupied, I have invented a new pastime — mapping what I call the underbelly of the hotel. Every public feature of this hotel has a corresponding private one. Like the glittery elevators that clients use. They share the same shaft as the staff elevators, which are gray wooden boxes. These are accessible in hidden hallways that parallel the hotel hallways. To get into them you have to go through handleless doors that are made to blend into the maroon-striped wallpaper.

I've been mapping out these sorts of connections all week. I plan to show them to Danny, who's coming home from Cornwall on Thursday.

"Do you know Danny? He lives a few houses over?" I ask Margie on the way to work that morning.

"Sure. Well, I know his mother anyways."

"He's coming home today, from Cornwall."

"Hey, I didn't know you had a boyfriend." Margie tickles me in the ribs as she says this. The word sounds odd. It's not one that I ever use. I'm not sure how I feel about seeing Danny again. We haven't seen each other since that last night on the mountain, and it wasn't exactly a great night out. Danny barely spoke to me all the way home.

"I don't know if I'd call him that," I respond, embarrassed.

"How long's it been since you saw him?"

"About two months, I guess, since the end of summer."

"You come over later, I'll do your hair up special, okay?" Margie winks. I recall sitting on the old washing machine watching Margie twist and pull my mother's hair into funny shapes, or dying it different colours.

"Okay, I guess," I say hesitantly. The whole notion of fussing with my hair strikes me as odd. I'm the sort of person who usually just pulls her hair back in a ponytail, no fuss.

When Yurek and my father have finally settled in front of the TV after supper, I leave by my bedroom window. I wonder how my father would react if he realized that he has forgotten that today is my eighteenth birthday. I'm legal now, whatever that means. It doesn't surprise me that my father doesn't know, since it was my mother who always arranged cakes and presents. I'm kind of relieved because if Yurek knew, he'd want to do something big. I can just see him buying party hats and blowers for us to wear and play with, he's so clueless. I was kind of thinking that my mother might be waiting for today to get in touch with me. That would explain why she waited so long. Maybe she wanted it to be a birthday present. But nothing came in the mail and no one's called. I guess she's forgotten too.

I'm not even sure if I'm going to tell Danny.

A few minutes later, I'm sitting in Margie's living room. She stands behind me, her own hair twisted and pulled into a bun, black cream smothering her face with holes around her eyes, nose and mouth. She tells me it's a mud facial and I nod, as if I've seen one before. I'm the type of person who brushes her teeth, washes her face with a hot cloth and brushes her hair once in the mornings. Anything else would seem superfluous.

"Now, what should we do?" Margie holds my hair up to one side then the other, trying to decide.

"Something plain, nothing fancy," I respond. I can't imagine meeting Danny in the back lane with my hair twisted and curled. He'd probably laugh.

Margie settles on washing it and setting it in big rollers. Then she makes me sit under the helmet-like dryer with the long wrinkly neck. I must look like an odd creature from outerspace, or an alien character in *Star Trek*, one that Captain Kirk has to battle.

I can barely hear a word, but Margie keeps talking anyway, chewing her gum and occasionally throwing her head back to laugh. She holds both hands up, fingers spread, to indicate ten more minutes. Then she disappears into her bedroom. While she's gone, I occupy myself by looking through some photo albums in her bookcase. I have to duck out from under the helmet to reach them. Most of the shots are of a younger Margie, at birthday parties and trips to the beach. I stop at a picture of five girls, their arms linked. They've been captured with their legs in mid-air, as though they're doing the cancan. They're all wearing tight cut-offs and sweaters and their hair is cut short and curly. I recognize Margie right away, because of the way her mouth is open in obvious laughter. The girl beside her is throwing her head back toward one shoulder like a model. She looks like a girl who might go anywhere or do anything, her expression is so confident. I see her pirouetting off the paper and into a fantastic future. The longer I stare at this girl, the more familiar her features become. I almost gasp when it hits me that it is my mother.

I peel the plastic back carefully and lift out the picture. Then I slip it into the back pocket of my jeans. I duck back out and replace the album. Later, Margie comes back out and snaps off the dryer, and everything is quiet again.

"Well, whad'ya think, kid?" Margie holds up the curls and lets them fall to my shoulders.

I think that now would be a good time to ask Margie about my mother, about before she married my father, when she was still Anna. I can't recall anyone at home calling her Anna. I called her Mom, and my father didn't really call her anything. If he wanted to talk to her she was usually there, in sight. If the phone was for her he'd just say, "it's for you."

My father must have used the name Anna at some point. I try to imagine him proposing, slipping the word "Anna" in at the end of his sentence, but I can't. I also can't picture the moment of my birth, eighteen years ago, the two of them peering down at me, aglow. Anyway, that scene is straight out of a diaper commercial.

"Well, do you like it or not, kid?" Margie asks again.

"It's great, thanks." I say this but don't believe it. I feel unnatural. And I'm afraid that Danny will wonder why I've gone to such trouble. He once said that was what he liked about me, that I wasn't fussy. "There aren't many girls you could take to a boxcar," he once said. I wasn't sure how I should feel about that, but I suppose he meant it as a compliment.

I leave Margie's and descend her front stairs, the curls bouncing awkwardly on my shoulders.

Chapter 15

I wind my way around to the back lane where I've arranged to meet Danny. He's wearing an army jacket, the kind made of material that looks like a green and brown jigsaw puzzle. He sure doesn't need any camouflage in this gray lane. There's hardly any foliage, even in the summer, apart from our maple tree.

Danny looks bigger than before, as though he's been inflated. He's starting to look like the other men in his family, or at least what I can remember of his father and uncle. The two of them used to sit out on chairs that they'd bring home from their furniture shop, chairs that had been reupholstered but never claimed. They always seemed to loom high over the backs of these chairs, their butts squeezed into them, as though the chairs had been made for dolls.

"Hey, you're looking good," Danny says, picking up a curl and letting it fall.

We stand apart, looking one another over. "Why'd you shave your head?" I ask.

"Well, why not? I figured it'd keep the grease and oil off."

"Let's get out of here," I say. "Do you still have a car?"

"No. It broke down in Cornwall, or Corn-hole as I should call it. What a dump! I got a lift in. Guess we'll have to stick close to home."

"Why didn't you fix it?" Danny just shrugs, as if he has no explanation. I'm disappointed, but try not to let it show. We head off down the lane and end up behind the Catholic church. We descend the back stairs, avoiding the small puddles where the autumn rain has gathered.

"Haven't been here for a while," Danny remarks. "Cigarette?" He pulls two out, lights them both then hands one over.

"So, what have you been up to in Cornwall?" I ask.

"Helping out in the garage. A lot of hard work though."

"Oh really, like what? Pumping gas and washing windshields?"

"Very funny. There's way more to it than that. I told you I learned about brakes. I'm supposed to get into the exhaust system next, when my cousin gets a chance." After a pause Danny asks me if I like my job.

"It's okay," I answer. "A lot of hard work though."

"Oh ya, like making beds and scrubbing toilets, right? Bet you see a lot of hanky panky, eh? All that between-the-sheets stuff?"

"No," I snap. Danny would think of that first. "In fact, I don't see much of anything, except unmade beds and dirty bathrooms."

"It's bloody freezing out here," says Danny. "Let's go in somewhere."

"Like where?" I ask.

"Too bad we can't go back to our suite, eh?" Danny nudges me with his elbow. "I bet you forgot about our suite?"

"No, I haven't forgotten," I say. How could I ever forget making out in a boxcar?

"I know where we can go, I think. Come on," I say suddenly, pulling Danny's arm.

Margie greets us in her housecoat, her hair tucked under a kerchief, her skin still wet from the water that has washed off the mud facial. She's patting her face gently with a hand towel.

"Sorry, Margie. We just wanted somewhere to hang out for a while. We can't go to my place and Danny's mother is home." Margie tells us we can stay as late as we want but that she has to get some sleep. Then she reminds me how early we both have to get up in the morning.

"There's some Coke in the fridge if you want it. See you." Margie waves and disappears behind her bedroom door.

Danny and I sit on the floral sofa. It's so soft I feel as though I'm sinking and I really have to work to shift my weight. The sofa is covered in pillows that are piled up like sandbags, keeping back some sort of tidal wave, between us. Danny is already picking them up one by one and dropping them on the floor as he moves closer.

He puts his arm around me. It seems heavier than I remember. He kisses me and I try to respond, but the sound of Margie coughing distracts me.

"Not as private as our suite," Danny jokes. When Margie is quiet we begin to kiss again. This time Danny begins to unbutton my shirt.

"We can't do this here," I protest, holding my shirt together.

"Ah, come on," Danny says. "Margie won't mind. She's cool."

"Danny, she's my mother's friend." I say, pulling myself as upright as the sofa will allow.

"So what's she going to do? Tell her?" Danny says this as if he thinks she really can. Has he forgotten that my mother has vanished? "Hey, wasn't one of the *X*s over here? Maybe we could do some snooping around after Margie's lights go out."

"Danny, for God's sake. Can't you give that map a rest. It's gone, burned, remember?"

"Come on, Sandra, don't worry," Danny says, trying to kiss me again. "I haven't seen you for ages."

I try to kiss him back, but I still feel weird with Margie right behind her bedroom door.

"Think of it as an adventure," Danny says. I

know I've heard these words before, first in that horrid tunnel that we drove through to get to the canal, and later in the boxcar.

"You think everything's an adventure," I respond.

"That's right," Danny says, smiling. And then he's all over me, kissing me and groping me, undoing my clothes beneath him. I bat at him with my free hand, resisting the urge to scream into his ear. I can't believe he's trying to make out with me so quickly. We barely even talked. I feel I don't know him anymore.

"Danny, let go!" I hiss into his ear, pushing against him with all my might.

"Spoilsport," Danny says with a sigh, rolling off me. "What else is there to do?"

I know it would be futile to suggest having a conversation. We never did have many of those. And what's there to talk about anyway?

"Forget it," I say. Then I get up and march down the hall to Margie's bathroom. I sit on the closed toilet seat, head in my hands, trying to figure out what to do next. I brought him here, now I'll have to get him out of here. My head is pounding. I need to find some Aspirin. I open Margie's medicine cabinet. The two bottom shelves contain only one thing: mini-soaps from the hotel. They're stacked like bricks, some of their covers so old they've yellowed. One bar sits alone, amidst Margie's eyeliner pencils and mascara bottles on the top shelf. There's some writing on it. I pick it up and read Room 701 written in black ink. 701 is a room I've never cleaned. I wonder why Margie would have wanted to remember it.

When I rejoin Danny, he's smoking, totally oblivious to the mess that we've made. I pick up the pillows and throw them forcefully back onto the sofa. Danny doesn't even notice that I'm angry. He's teasing me, kicking my behind with his foot as I bend.

"For God's sake, Danny, will you just cut it out," I snap, in as loud a whisper as I can. I'm sure that Margie is up, listening to all this, cursing me for bringing Danny here and making so much noise.

"What are you so hot about?" he asks. I don't answer. I'm too angry to even look at him anymore, and yet I can't seem to tell him why I'm angry. It's just like between me and my father. I feel the anger, yet I can't seem to tell him why I'm angry. It's all too hard to untangle or explain. The anger is just there, like a solid wall, one that you can't get around but can't break into understandable pieces either.

"Come on, we'd better go," I say finally, straightening the pillows one last time.

"I'm not going back," Danny tells me as we near my house. "To Cornwall I mean."

"Why not?"

"I'm sick of my cousin," Danny says angrily. "He makes me do all the crap jobs." I wonder about changing brake pads and exhaust systems.

Was that true? Something about the way Danny's hanging his head so low stops me from asking him. "I'm going to look for a better job here," he continues. "Maybe you could ask Margie if she could get me something at the hotel. I could work with you. That'd be fun. We could fool around in all those empty rooms," Danny says, grinning. He really just doesn't get it.

"So, will you ask her for me?" he says. I don't want to do it, but I just can't think of a way to say no. How would I explain it? I shrug and mutter okay.

When we get to the bottom of my stairs, Danny puts his hand on my arm. I pull it away and, without even saying goodbye, turn and haul myself up onto my window ledge and climb in.

When I'm safe inside my room, I pull out my homemade map of the hotel, the one that I planned to show Danny. I'm glad I didn't let him see it. I realize now that the last thing Danny needs is another map, especially now that he's home again and has nowhere else to go. And what if Margie did find him a job? He'd be hauling me all over the hotel, following this new map. It'd be like summer all over again, chasing down all those useless Xs.

I spread the map on my bed. I grab a pen from my dresser and quickly mark an X approximately where room 701 would be. For some reason, this feels like a birthday gift, of sorts.

Chapter 16

By November, my job has become dull. The only thing that breaks the routine is when I'm wrongly accused of stealing. A man from Chicago claims that he hid an expensive ring in his pillowcase and that I must have stolen it. Later that day he finds it in his shaving kit. He follows me around for a while, trying to chat. He keeps saying how sorry he is and can he make it up to me by taking me out. I tell him that isn't necessary but he stations himself in front of my cart, bracing it. He's wearing a gold ring on every finger and I wonder if the lost ring ever really existed, or if it was just an excuse to start hitting on me. I turn away to get more supplies from the linen closet and continue to ignore him until my coldness finally gets through to him.

One day, out of the blue, Danny shows up at the hotel. I haven't seen him in two weeks. He was back in Cornwall, getting the rest of his stuff. I was kind of hoping he'd change his mind and stay there.

"How did you find me?" I ask.

"It wasn't hard. I just walked up and down each floor until I found you. There's no law against coming here, you know." Neither of us speaks for a minute, and then Danny says, "So, did you ask Margie about the job yet?"

"Ya, I did. She said there's nothing," I lie. I never even mentioned it to Margie. Why should I? Let Danny find his own job.

"So, you gonna let me into a room or what?" Danny asks.

"I can't do that. I'll get fired."

"Ah, don't be such a chicken. No one'll know."

"But Danny ..." Next thing I know he's pulling my arm and leading me toward the room I just came out of. I give up and tell him he can hang out, if he keeps the TV on very low, until twelve, which is one hour before check-in time.

Danny hangs out at the hotel all week and into the next, watching dumb game shows, like the *Price is Right* and *Family Feud*. I'm really scared that one of the other maids is going to notice and report me. It's not like he just stays in the room either. He's always popping out of the room I've told him to stay in, trying to entice me inside. I'm running out of ways to say no.

One day Danny starts going on about this bar he discovered in the lobby, one that looks really cool. I know which one he means — the Wa-Tika, a tropical bar. I put a brochure about it in each check-out room. He wants us to go there for lunch.

"How the hell can we do that?" I ask, hoping he'll drop the subject. "I'm in uniform. Besides, the chambermaids aren't allowed in there. I was told that the day I was hired."

"You could get changed in a room before we go. No one'll know," Danny responds.

"Forget it, Danny. I'm not doing it." But he keeps bringing it up, every time he comes. I now cringe whenever I see him saunter down the hallway. I'd hide, but it's kind of hard. I'm practically attached to this big cart that gives away my location.

One day, Danny shows me a gym bag full of spare clothes. "They'll be easy to slip over your uniform," he says. "Big jeans and sweatshirt. I even brought a baseball cap, to cover up your hair."

"Danny, read my lips," I say. "NO. I'm not doing it. I don't want to lose my job."

"You're no bloody fun anymore," Danny snaps. Then, before I can react, he grabs me around the waist and throws me onto the bed. "It'll be more comfortable than our boxcar," he says.

"Danny, let go. I have to get back to work," I protest, trying to loosen the grip he has on me.

"Screw your job!" Danny shouts, scaring me. He's still holding my arm, twisting it in a painful way. "All you care about is your job. It's a pathetic job anyway. Anybody could do it."

It hits me as Danny's yelling that that's his problem — I have a job and he doesn't. That's why he's so determined to make me lose mine.

I try to use the momentum from the springiness of the bed to push myself up and regain my footing. I'm almost there, when Danny lunges at me with his free hand, grabbing my other arm. Next thing I know he pins me to the bed and tries to kiss me.

That's when I lose it. I free one of my knees, flex it quickly, and jab him in the groin. Danny gasps, doubles up and rolls onto the floor.

"Get the hell out of here, you loser!" I yell down at him. "And don't come back. My job may be pathetic, but you're even more pathetic." I'm shaking from head to toe. I run into the bathroom and lock the door.

I pray that he'll leave now. I hear him getting up, sighing as if he's still in pain. His footsteps stop outside the bathroom door. "You bitch," he mutters, his voice faint. I must have really kicked him hard. Finally I hear the door bang shut. As it does, I hear my father's words replay in my mind. "Danny's a bum, just a bum."

My God! How could he get it so right?

Chapter 17

I haven't been able to put room 701 out of my mind. I keep hoping it'll be part of my daily run, but my runs seem to skirt around it. If I'm assigned other rooms on the seventh floor, I venture down the hall, hoping to pop inside 701 on some pretext while the maid is cleaning it and the door is open, but my timing is always off. Besides, what excuse could I use? I never speak to anyone, and the supply closets are well-stocked with anything I could possibly need.

I'll need to get the key from the key wall in the basement, but how? Then I remember that I saw an old key in my mother's junk drawer the day I was looking for her aunt's address in the summer. It was a similar style to the keys on the wall. Maybe I could use it as a decoy, swap it with the original. I look for it again one night, when my father is out and I find it. I have no idea which door it opens. My mother has only had two addresses in her whole life — the flat across the street that she grew up in and this one. Well, I suppose she now has an address somewhere, but this key couldn't be related to it, not unless she snuck back one night and slipped the key in her drawer. Maybe if I hold it in my hand an address will begin to form, the way a clairvoyant can hold an object and lead the police to a criminal.

I decide that a Thursday would be the best day to attack room 701. It's payday and that means fewer people milling about the basement. A lot of the maids leave their key belts in the office and run out to do their banking or shopping during the forty-five minute lunch break. Most of the office employees, who get an hour, also disappear. The one or two employees who stay behind are hidden in the back office behind the key wall. If I can go in and out fast enough, I'll be able to switch keys unnoticed. That's my plan.

It takes two weeks before I work up enough nerve to execute my plan. That payday, I wait fifteen minutes at the bottom of the stairwell, eating my ham sandwich which I have carried in the pocket of my apron all morning. Hardly anyone uses this stairwell. It's really a fire exit. It's kind of airless and soundproof, and when I'm sitting in it I imagine I'm in some sort of solitary confinement. But I feel safe down here. No one can get to me. If I could, I'd spend the whole day hiding. I keep expecting Danny to show up, to confront me about what happened. I keep remembering the look on his face when he pushed me on the bed. I can't believe I had the nerve to do what I did.

When I've finished my sandwich, I open the door slowly and peek out. Just as I suspected, the hallway is empty. I saunter over casually and startle the chip-lady at the canteen. She has to put down her *National Enquirer* to serve me. Then I tiptoe down the hall and open the door to the office as quietly as I can. I have squished the bag of chips into my apron pocket and removed the key that I brought from home. Luckily, no one is at the front desk. The seventh row of keys is about a foot above my head, and I have no trouble slipping 701 from its hook and hanging my mother's key in its place. No one steps out from behind the wall to ask me any questions. If anyone heard me, they probably figured I was just a maid returning or picking up my key belt.

I run up the fourteen flights to the seventh floor, stopping only once to catch my breath. I knock lightly on the door before entering, just in case. Inside, I face a room that looks like dozens of others in the hotel, with a mismatched bedspread and curtains in bright, loud colours. The double bed is impeccably made. The bathroom sparkles, towels and face cloths symmetrically placed on their bars. The work of one of the older maids, no doubt, maybe even Valérie. All the dust has been removed, the lint vacuumed. The empty hangers in the closet have one perfect inch of space between them. If this room once held meaning for Margie, it was for events that have left no trace. What was I expecting to find anyway? My mother, propped up on pillows with a glass of champagne? Why did I think she'd be connected to this hotel somehow? Just because the number was on a piece of soap at Margie's, her closest friend? Is this what is known as clutching at straws?

Besides, if my mother was here, Margie would have told me. And if she didn't want me to know, she never would have gotten me this job.

Before leaving, I open the top drawer of the dresser. In it I find a hotel pad and pen, and several brochures on roomservice and other hotel features, nothing out of the ordinary.

I pick up the Wa-Tika brochure. It's the same one that I too place in the top right drawer of each checkout room, but I usually do so automatically, without really looking. The photographer has managed to make the bar look polished and exotic. Happy customers sit in coconut chairs, a bamboo-and-palm-leaf ceiling above them, colourful drinks in the shells of pineapples on tables in front of them. On closer inspection, however, I notice that, sitting at a back table, unmistakable with her blond head thrown back, is Margie. Beside her, offering only a profile, is a woman with shoulder-length red hair. The face is small, too small to identify without hesitation, but the hair is very much like my mother's.

I turn the brochure over, looking for a date, but there isn't one. The Wa-Tika has probably looked the same for decades. The customers' clothes are so eclectic that they offer no clue of the time. Margie hasn't changed her hairstyle since I was a kid, and the red-haired woman is wearing a black sweater. What year would that signify?

I look at my watch. I've stayed too long. Lunch is now over, and I won't be able to return the key without being seen. Before leaving, I stuff the brochure inside my apron pocket. Even though my own cart is loaded with Wa-Tika brochures, I can't be sure they're all the same.

The maid whose run I've just invaded is turning her cart into the hallway just as I pull open the stairwell door. I run down to the fourth floor and resume my place behind my own cart. I finish my rooms at a frantic pace, vacuuming carpets I would normally just ignore, ridding myself of excess energy. The key to 701 slaps my belly inside my pocket as I jerk the hose back and forth around the green and orange squares. I finish my entire run one hour earlier than usual. There is nothing to do now but sit in the supply closet on a stack of extra blankets, study the brochure, and wait until it's time to clock out. I can't believe I'm actually leaving the hotel with a key to a room in my possession. That would definitely get me fired.

Later that day, I'm halfway down the street when I notice a crowd gathered on the sidewalk just beyond my house, the red flash of a light pulsing somewhere just beyond it. I freeze for a minute, then continue slowly. I've had enough surprises for one day. I can see Danny there, standing beside his mother, who only stands to his shoulders. I haven't seen her outside her house for ages.

I stand back, not wanting Danny to see me. "They'll probably find that dog in there too somewhere, cut up in the freezer or something," one of the neighbours is saying. "Or down in the basement," someone else offers. So, it's the weirdo next door, Siberia's master.

For a second, I remember the way Danny reversed down the lane so that I could liberate Siberia, no questions asked. That was such a kind gesture. Could I have I misread him at the hotel? Is he really such a bad guy, or is he just reacting to his circumstances in a bad way? If his father had never left and if he could find some direction in his life, would he actually make a good boyfriend?

But then Danny turns to the neighbour and says, "Ya, he probably used a chainsaw, the freak!" It's as though he's completely forgotten the truth, as though the summer never happened. Then Danny's mother looks over at me and I can see how tired she looks. She can't be more than fifty, but she looks about seventy-five. She looks like one of those wrinkled apple dolls they sell at craft stores. She smiles at me and I try to smile back. Then she does something really strange. She steps back and bends toward me, where Danny can't see, and whispers, "It's okay, dear, you should go on now." Her voice is so soft I think I may have imagined her words. I don't really know what she's telling me, but suddenly I see my life as it would be if Danny and I had stayed together. We'd get married, then I'd get pregnant and we'd struggle for money and end up living here forever. It's the story of my mother's life, almost, and the story of Danny's mother's life. Even Margie, who has no kids, never really left here. Is that what she means by "you should go on?"

But it won't happen, I remind myself. I'm saving money, I'm getting out.

I back away and enter my flat. From the porch window I watch two men carry out the stretcher. A white sheet covers the body underneath. Oddly, the crowd doesn't disperse. Maybe people really are waiting to see if they find the dog.

"So, the old fool finally kicked the bucket," my father remarks that night at supper, sticking his chin out in the direction of the house next door. His remark is not directed at anyone, but to the air between us.

"Maybe he died of a broken heart," I respond. "Maybe he never got over the disappearance of his dog." I watch my father's reaction closely. My mother's disappearance should have laid him out on a stretcher like that. I feel like pulling out the Wa-Tika brochure and dangling it in his face, just to take an extra shot at him. But then he shrugs and looks down in a way that almost makes me regret having said it. And Yurek, who would normally seize any opportunity to draw the two of us into conversation, doesn't even look up. He's too busy sucking the remaining bits of chicken off the bones on his plate.

Chapter 18

All the following week I try to put the Wa-Tika brochure out of my mind, but I can't. Especially since my cart is loaded with a fresh stack of them every morning. I now feel very strange stuffing a picture of what could be my mother into the musty-smelling drawers of the old bureaus. It's as though I'm shoving her away, into some dark unpopular place, the same shady place that my father has obviously put her in, that I too had put her in. I mean, it's not as though I've been knocking myself out trying to find her. Although, I have to keep reminding myself, she's not exactly killing herself to let me know where she is either.

Yurek has now officially moved into the spare room in the front. Now he and my father rise at the same time in the mornings, and mine is the third cup to hit the white sink. I don't like it, but there's nothing I can do. I have three months' salary saved up now, though, so I won't be around much longer.

In the meantime, I've decided that I need to get into the Wa-Tika.

One night, when my father is down in his cellar, I approach Yurek. I hate myself for doing it, but I can't think of anyone else to ask. I can't picture myself walking into a bar on my own. I'd be too noticeable, plus I've never done it. And I can't ask Danny — not now. He'd only gloat about wanting to take me there in the first place. Besides, I doubt he'd forgive me for that knee in the groin. Yurek's my only choice.

"Yurek. Would you do me a big favour. I want to go somewhere and I need your help." Yurek flashes me a broad and eager smile. I knew he'd go for the part about being helpful.

"It might have something to do with my mother," I say, although I don't know if I really believe this. After all, a bar of soap and an unidentifiable picture in a brochure aren't really solid clues. Yurek is beaming, picturing the happy reunion, no doubt. I explain where and when to meet me, and we both instinctively know to change the subject when my father comes back into the kitchen, his bottle tucked securely under his arm.

I spend all week planning Friday night. I'm going to have to leave the hotel the same way I do every night, standing in line with the other maids, purses open for inspection. I'll have to wait until I'm beyond that point to don my disguise. That means I'm going to have to bring the clothes I'll change into to work Friday morning. I hope Margie won't pry about the bag and its contents. I'm normally empty-handed. The pièce de résistance of my disguise will be the wig that I found in my mother's junk drawer. It has short, straight black hair. I don't know how I'll explain it to Yurek, but I'll think of something.

On my way out of the hotel that Friday, when I open my purse for inspection, I spy the wig curled up inside like a sleeping animal. I hurry around the block, wading through the slush of a December snowfall and dodging the spray of rush-hour traffic. It's already dark out and hundred of shoppers are racing around with bags hanging from their wrists. Christmas shopping, I suppose. An old lady ringing a bell beside a Salvation Army bubble looks right into my eyes and smiles, as if she's sure I'm going to give her something. But I don't stop. I have a more important mission.

I lock myself in a cubicle and strip down. I pull on my new dress, my one and only indulgent purchase with my hotel wages, and bunch my old clothes into the bag. It's hard to put the wig on without a mirror, but I've practised several times at home, and can do most of it by touch. Luckily, no one is at the gold-framed mirror in the parlour. Here, I put some final touches to the wig, then dab on some eyeshadow and lipstick. Eventually, a few other women enter the parlour, taking up seats beside me in front of the long mirror. I try to look casual, as though I've done this many times before. They don't give me funny looks, so I assume that the wig looks natural. Anyway, in the dim light of the bar it won't be noticed.

I leave the washroom, bag in hand, wishing I could sneak through the hidden employee doors and deposit my junk on the other side. Yurek is leaning against the registration desk, where I told him to meet me. I walk up behind him and tap him on the shoulder. He turns to look down and it takes him a few seconds to realize it's me.

"You are looking unusual," he says, confused.

"Thank you, Yurek," I respond as casually as I can, to make everything seem ordinary. Then he smiles and I realize he probably thinks I went through all this trouble just for him. I suddenly remember all those compliments he likes to pay me and I hope he doesn't get the wrong idea about tonight. We cross the lobby to the tropical bar, passing between the fake palm trees that sit like guards on either side. Inside, I lead Yurek to a table way in the back, one that gives a view of the entire bar. The seats really are shaped like hollowed-out coconuts. Matted straw covers the walls up to the ceiling, which is covered with plastic palm leaves. Stuck into the walls and ceiling are tropical paraphernalia — starfish, shells, pineapples, and mangoes. The air smells of incense, one last-ditch attempt to add to its exotic atmosphere. Santana music is blaring in the background. It's not exactly tropical, but it's probably more exotic than The Rolling Stones.

It occurs to me that my father would call this place *ersatz*, a word he uses to describe anything fake. He once said that his childhood had been full of *ersatz* — fake coffee, eggs, and chocolate. Substitutions, like he was supposed to be right now for my mother.

Our table is lit by a flower-shaped candle floating in a red dish. When Yurek spreads out his hands on the table I notice that they're covered in cuts and callouses, signs of work in the bottle factory, I guess. I'm not sure what his job is, exactly. Probably packaging. I've never noticed his hands before.

We order our drinks, then sit silently. I don't have much to say to Yurek. I wonder when he's going to ask me to explain how this excursion relates to my mother. But finally he breaks the ice by talking about my father.

"Everyone very happy to have your father back at work, Sandra. He's good man. He helps people."

I have a hard time picturing my father helping people, although I know his disputes were with management, not his co-workers. "Try to compromise," I remember my mother saying, but he didn't have the temperament for compromise, or obedience. Still, he was a good technician and could fix machines that remained mysterious to others. During a bad spell he'd talk about sabotage, how easy it would be. A snip-snip here and a snip-snip there. My mother would worry, afraid to ask when he got home. *Ersatz* men, I even remember him calling his bosses.

As Yurek continues talking about my father, the bar fills with familiar faces. Margie and a group of women — one of them the woman that hired me, another the one who outfitted me — settle down at a table in the corner to the left. None of them are chambermaids — otherwise they wouldn't be allowed in here.

"Your father refuse to be union leader," Yurek is saying. "We ask him many times because he is a good man and he can fight well. But he refuse. He say organizations are all corrupt. He has experience, you know, in the war."

I take a deep breath and pray he won't start telling war stories again. I wish he'd quit distracting me from my mission, which is to try to locate the exact set-up of the brochure picture. I'm pretty sure I have identified the table. It's definitely the one Margie and her gang are at. Once I'm sure of the set-up, I plan to show the brochure to the waiter and ask if he knows who the red-haired woman in the black sweater is.

"And he was very brave. You don't know, in this country, what it means to stand up to such authority. But your father, he knows. And such a man would be a good union leader."

"Why don't you lead your union, Yurek? You must have experience too," I ask, trying to divert him from my father.

"No, no. Not like your father. He work fifteen years there."

I order another coconut rum drink. It fills me

114

with a warm, woozy feeling, as though my body is melting into the chair. The bar fills with more and more people. Margie's table is now so crowded they have pulled a few extra chairs over. It's obvious that Margie knows just about everyone in this place. I realize that the man who is pulling a chair up to her table is the guard who inspects our purses after a shift.

"Your father, he miss your mother very much, you know." Yurek reaches for my hand across the round table as he says this. I laugh as I instinctively pull my hand back. It seems as though the laugh goes on forever, floating through the air long after my mouth is closed. Yurek looks crushed.

"It's very hard for your father … because of what happened to his sister, you know?" I look at him. No, I don't know. I have no idea what he's going on about now. What does my aunt have to do with anything? I barely remember her, except that she seemed really sour. "He feel very bad what happened to her in the war."

Oh, God. Now he's going to explain. But I don't want to hear it. And I have to go to the bathroom really badly. Maybe if I get up he'll shut up.

"His mother blame him. But it's not his fault she gets hurt. He can't get her into the hole in cellar." I can't believe he's talking about the cellar. How does he even know about it? It's the last place I want to think about right now. I'm already feeling a bit queasy. I guess I'm not used to drinking.

"Yurek, I really need to go to the bathroom, okay?"

On the way to the bathroom, I notice that the woman sitting alone at the bar is the one I helped escape through the basement of the hotel many months ago. The bar is rimmed by a glass tube with real fish swimming inside it. She seems to be following the fish as they dart around under her arms.

The door marked Ladies is just past the table that Margie and her gang are at. What if they recognize me? I'm well disguised and I don't feel at all like myself. I even change my walk, adding a bit more wiggle to my stride. I make it there all right, but after I'm finished, just as I'm stepping out of my cubicle the woman who hired me walks in. She looks at me for what seems like a long time, but says nothing. I leave quickly, without stopping to wash my hands.

I grab my coat and, without even telling Yurek what's happening, quickly exit the bar to the hotel lobby. It is so brightly lit after the darkness of the bar that I feel I've been captured by a spotlight, like an animal that has wandered out onto the highway. My only hope is that I can find the door that leads to the hidden hallway from the main lobby. I must duck into it discreetly, if I do find it, which I do. It blends into the wallpaper as it does on all the other floors. Only it's locked. I keep pushing at it, desperate to be able to vanish inside and hide.

When I turn the corner, Yurek is standing there, looking forlorn.

"Why do you leave?" he asks.

"I felt sick. I wanted some air. I think we'd better go home now, Yurek." I wonder how that word "home" would sound if anyone heard me. They'd think we lived together, which I guess we do.

We stand on the curb and Yurek sticks his hand up to hail a taxi. It sprays us with slush as it screeches to a stop and we have to jump over a puddle to get in. Yurek must be wondering why I invited him. I'm beginning to wonder myself. What was the point of this mission? Was I hoping to see my mother walk into the Wa-Tika just because her picture may have been in a brochure? Or, did I really think the waiter would be able to identify some random woman in a brochure? We're halfway home when I remember, with a gasp, that I left my bag of everyday clothes under our table at the Wa-Tika. I'll never get it back now.

The taxi pulls up to the house and I look around to make sure no one is there to see us getting out of it together. "We should go in separately, Yurek, or my father might see us."

"Your father is sleeping for sure," Yurek says confidently.

"He might not be, Yurek. You don't know everything." I turn toward my bedroom window. I'm kind of sorry that he'll now learn about my secret hatch, but I really don't want to walk in through the front door with him.

In my room, I take off the wig and throw it on the floor, where it curls up like a cat. I take some cream and tissue and wipe off my makeup, then I change into my pyjamas. There! There's no trace of the other me left. I'll need to use the toilet before going to sleep. I haven't heard any signs of life out there, but you never know. I'd hate to run into my father now.

I step out of my room cautiously. All clear. But then just as I'm starting up the hallway, a hand grabs my arm from behind. For a split second I think it's my father, but when the arm spins me around, I see that it's Yurek. He pulls me toward him. I try to wiggle free, but I can't. He's much stronger than I am.

"Let go of me," I snap.

But he's already bending down and trying to plant a wet kiss on my mouth. It's as though I'm watching him bend and bend forever, in slow motion. When his mouth touches mine I twist away, but then he just starts kissing my cheek. I kick him and he stops for a second, but my arms are still pinned back. I work on filling my mouth with enough saliva to spit in his face, but just as I'm about to hawk, my father's door opens. We both freeze. My father steps out into the hallway in his pyjamas. He looks from me to Yurek several times. For a split second I'm terrified that he'll misread the situation and think I've invited this somehow. But my fingers are arched like claws, and my mouth is open and the spit is sitting there,

ready to fly. These signs should tell him something. But then it occurs to me that Yurek is his
friend, his best friend, more like a son to him than
I am a daughter. Of course he'll side with him.

"Dad, help me, please," I say. My voice is so
low I'm not even sure he can hear me. He just
stands there staring at me. For a second I'm afraid
that he's so drunk he won't be able to move. What
if he collapses in a heap, just when I need him
most? But then his eyes brighten, like a florescent
light bursting on. His usual faraway stare, the one
that has been there ever since my mother left, van-
ishes.

"What the hell are you doing?" my father
shouts. I have no idea who he's talking to. Probably me. But when he steps closer I can see it's
Yurek he's staring at.

"Nothing," Yurek says. He has let go of my arm
and is backing up. My skin burns where he was
squeezing.

"Sandra?" my father asks. I don't know what to
say. What if Yurek tells my father I asked him out?
He'll blame all this on me for sure. He might even
call me a slut again.

"He was trying to kiss me," I answer. It isn't a
lie. It is what was happening. The rest of the
evening has nothing to do with it.

Next thing I know, my father grabs Yurek by
the collar of his shirt and pulls him toward his
room. "Pack up," he says. "I want you gone in the
morning. You can't stay here anymore."

Then my father returns to where I'm standing, frozen with surprise. "He won't ever bother you again," he says, just like that, matter-of-factly. Then he returns to his room and he doesn't close his door. I forget about the bathroom, run into my bedroom, lock the door, and try to sleep. I have an incredible feeling that something big happened tonight. My mind keeps replaying the scene in the hallway, until eventually I doze off.

In the morning, the house is extremely quiet, even for a Saturday. Then I remember. My father had to catch a train to Toronto early this morning for his training course. He must have gotten ready extra quietly, to let me rest.

And Yurek must be gone too. Gone because my father kicked him out — for trying to kiss me. My father must not have wanted to leave me alone with Yurek while he was away. That means he was scared for my safety. I find this incredible. I just lie in my bed thinking about it for ages. My father, choosing me over his friend, worrying about me getting hurt. I never would have thought it possible.

Chapter 19

At break time Monday morning I'm called into the office. Once again, I find myself sitting in front of the woman who hired me.

"Mademoiselle, you were seen wandering around on floors where you had no business. Is it true?" She holds her head tilted to one side as she tells me this, as though the weight of the reprimand has tipped it. I see no point in lying. I also see nothing wrong with being on another floor, so I nod.

"We do not allow floor-hopping here." It sounds like some new dance and for a minute I picture the old chambermaids in a long row, arms around each other's waists, just above their aprons, their muscular legs kicking out in unison.

"You are assigned your rooms and you are expected to stay there and not go travelling all around," she says, her mouth pinched and puckered. I still don't answer her. I'm too busy studying the key that hangs under number 701. It's silver and long just like the rest, but its head is oval instead of square. I wonder if anyone but me would notice this difference.

She keeps staring at me and when I don't flinch, she adds, "I am afraid we are going to have to let you go."

"Just because I was on a different floor?" I can't believe it. That was weeks ago.

"No, not only that. Mostly because of this," the woman says, pulling a familiar bag out from under her desk. It's the one I left at the Wa-Tika just three days ago. She hands it over the desk to me, holding it with only two fingers, as though it's contaminated. I deliberately tuck my hand into my apron pocket and finger the real key to 701. I'll never return it now. She dismisses me by waving her hand.

I climb the four floors to the employee locker room, my feet heavy on the stairs, the incriminating bag of clothes in my hand. Who cares anyway? It's a stupid job, not one I'd want to do forever. I wouldn't want to risk turning into one of these old maids. They're all cracked. The other day one was crawling around under a table in the locker room, biting other maids on the ankles. I thought I was going to be sick. That's what cleaning rooms for thirty years will do to you. I'm glad I'm leaving.

I stuff my uniform into my locker for the last time. But then, to make the job of finding it harder, I decide to hide it in the large bin in the corner of the room. As I'm throwing it over the rim, I notice that there are other items in the bin — hairbrushes, makeup, tangled pantyhose and empty deodorant bottles. And mine is not the only uniform abandoned in the bin. I wonder if the women who once wore them also left in a hurry; were they also fired, or did they leave in frustration, afraid of growing old and crazy here? I push the other uniforms aside. I want to bury mine deep. As I'm stuffing it inside, a white sheet of paper sticking out of an apron pocket catches my eye. I tug at it, releasing what looks like a picture. When I turn it over, I discover an image of myself as a child, standing under our maple tree, which is in full summer bloom.

I suck in my breath and freeze, completely stunned. How is this possible? Slowly, I hug the picture to my chest, cradling it there. I'm afraid to look again, in case I've seen wrong and the image is of someone else.

It's only when a drip lands on my hand that I realize I'm crying.

I exit the work area and descend to the hotel lobby in the client elevator. After all, I'm no longer an employee. I decide to walk home, along Sherbrooke Street and then up Park Avenue. It's a sunny and mild winter day, the kind of day where the snow is so bright it could blind you. Across Park Avenue, on Flanders Field, some men are kicking a soccer ball around, the air around them fogging when they exhale. At the bottom of Mount Royal, pigeons sit

flapping atop the green statues of heroes and hero-
ines, as though they're trying to lift them. I think
about the picture I just found. How did it come to be
in the hotel? There can only be one answer to that.
My mother must have worked there before me. I
remember my first day at the hotel, the way Margie
and the woman who hired me whispered behind my
back, the way the woman seemed to scrutinize my
face. Was Margie trying to reassure her that I would
be low risk? Had my mother done something wrong
to make the woman doubt me already? Had she
been caught off limits at the Wa-Tika too? And
Margie — what hand has she played in all this?

I pass the old YMCA where I used to do ballet,
spinning around like a butterfly while my mother
roamed around her favourite neighbourhood. I
remember one Saturday morning, when I came out
of ballet class and couldn't find her. I got dressed
and left the building. I found her up the street. She
was just standing still, looking down into the window of a basement flat. I tugged her purse to get
her attention, but she barely acknowledged me. I
looked into the apartment myself, trying to see
what she was so mesmerized by. All I saw was a
group of young people sitting around cross-legged
on the bare floor. One guy was strumming a guitar
and singing. Everyone else was swaying and clap-
ping. I had the feeling my mother wanted to be part
of that circle. It occurs to me now that she wasn't
that much older than they were.

Maybe she was planning her escape even then.

Chapter 20

When I get home, I spend a few minutes just walking up and down from room to room, as though I can't decide where to settle. There is so much restless energy in me, even after that long walk. And that picture? I can't stop thinking about it. My head is bursting with questions. I'll have to keep busy or I'll go nuts. I decide to clean, starting in my father's room. I get a bucket of soapy water and a dust rag and start scrubbing. Then I tackle the rest of the house, room by room, removing the layers of grime that have accumulated since I last cleaned in the summer. Then I do laundry, pulling dirty clothes out of the overflowing hamper in the bathroom and from various corners in my father's room and the kitchen. I've always hating doing laundry because our kitchen doesn't have proper hookups and I have to run the drainage hose down the hallway and stick it into the toilet. It's a miracle our house has never flooded. Next, in my own room, I tear down the cutesy posters from the walls and pack a box full of the childhood knick-knacks that lined my dresser. I rip off the frilly bordered bedspread that I yearned for when I was eight. When I'm done, I stand back and look around. It's still not perfect, but it sure is better. At least it doesn't scream childhood anymore.

I sit on my new plain bed and calculate my room count: six at the hotel this morning before my expulsion and now five more for a total of eleven. Not quite what I'm supposed to do in a day, but it'll have to do. It's almost six o'clock. That means Margie will be home. I know I have to face her and get some answers about my mother.

I take a deep breath before ringing her bell. As I wait for her to tug the string that runs down the banister to pull open the lock, I anticipate what she'll say. I expect that she'll deny knowing anything, like she did the first time I came here, almost a year ago.

"Can I come up?" I call into the dim stairwell once the door is open. I haven't been to Margie's since the night of my reunion with Danny. The sight of the sofa with its floral pillows brings it all back to me.

"Can we talk for a few minutes?"

"I was just getting supper," Margie says, which isn't really an answer.

I follow her into the familiar kitchen with its tall cupboards reaching up to the high ceiling. My mother would repaint the squares in ours from time to time, changing the color from orange to green to red, just for variety's sake, I suppose.

"I'm having spaghetti. Do you want some?" Margie asks hesitantly.

"No thanks. I've eaten." I sense she's nervous. She seems sterner than usual.

"I guess you know why I'm here," I say finally. I'm going to lead the conversation this time. Not like the last time I sat here, when she offered to find me work at the hotel, or the time before that, when I just stood helplessly at her front door asking if she knew where my mother was. Just in case she decides to play the innocent, I pull out the picture of me that I found at the hotel. "This was in an old apron on the fourth floor." I fix Margie with a glare that I wouldn't have dared use on her four months ago.

"Look, I don't know what to tell you. Your mother came to me as a friend. She said I was the only person she could trust. I couldn't very well go blabbing everything to you the minute her back was turned."

"Does that mean she doesn't want me to find her?"

"It means she doesn't want to be found. It has nothing to do with you," Margie replies. How can it have nothing to do with me? I remember playing hide-and-seek with my mother once when I was little. She crawled into a space that I never would have dreamed of hiding in, between the bathtub and sink. Eventually I gave up and called her, but she took her time to reappear. By the time she did, I was close to tears. She apologized and got me a bowl of ice cream to make up for it.

"Well, she's not at the hotel anymore, I take it, or I would have seen her," I say.

"She wasn't there long, only a few weeks. I helped fix it up with my friend on reception so that she could have a room for a while. It was off season, mid-winter, you know?"

"Room 701, by any chance?" Margie's eyes widen.

"How'd ya know?"

"Never mind." Let her be in the dark for a while, see how she likes it. "Then what?"

"Then I figured she might as well work and make a bit of cash, to help her out, until she got herself together."

"Together from what?"

"From life, kid. It has nothing to do with you."

"I wish you'd stop saying it has nothing to do with me. I'm her daughter!" I almost yell.

"But she left because she was unhappy with her life, with her marriage, not because of you. She said she just wanted to get on her feet, then she'd get in touch." So, if she hasn't been in touch yet that means she's still falling, gliding through the air like a cat with its paws poised for landing.

Margie eats her spaghetti, slurping it up as quietly as she can. Between bites she explains how my mother lived and worked at the hotel for a short while. But she left suddenly, which kind of made Margie look bad because she was the one who recommended her for the job. Just like with me, I think.

"What happened?"

"She got scared, one night at the bar. I'd talked her into coming, even though she wasn't supposed to. I knew it was forbidden for the chambermaids, but I felt sorry for her, cooped up alone in a small hotel room. I told her I'd smooth it over if she got caught. That night — bad luck, really — a photographer was taking shots for a new promotional brochure. It kind of freaked her out. She was afraid if anyone she knew saw it, they'd think she was having a good time. And she wasn't. She felt really bad about leaving you, trust me."

"But why did you get me the job at the hotel? Were you hoping I'd find her?"

"No … I don't know. Maybe. She was long gone by then. I thought I was helping you out."

"And did everyone know I was her daughter?" Maybe that's why the other maids treated me with such disdain.

"No. Only the woman who hired you." That explains her reluctance. I knew there was more to that story. "Sorry, kid."

"I'm not a kid, Margie."

"No, I guess you aren't."

"So, where is she now? I know you must know. You've probably known all along," I add. There's no way I'm going to trust her this time, not after everything that's happened. I can't believe she led me through that tiny door into the back of the hotel and walked me through those smelly hallways and never once had the urge to confess that she'd done the same thing with my mother.

Margie hesitates over her plate, staring at it intently, as though the lines that the spaghetti has left in the sauce are sending her some special message.

"She did give me something a while ago, in the summer. She met me downtown one day after work. She just showed up out of the blue really. She said she was getting settled, slowly. She wanted me to have her phone number, in case of an emergency. She said I should call if anything happened that she should know about. Or that I should give it to you if you really needed to get in touch with her."

Emergency? Didn't leaving me on my own constitute an emergency? I wonder what my mother's definition of "really needed" would be.

"She said she'd be sorry if something really bad happened and nobody could find her," Margie continues. Then she hands me a slip of paper. My skin burns where it touches me.

"You could have given it to me sooner. You knew I was worried," I spit at her. I can't believe she got me a job and did my hair but never told me that she knew how I could contact my mother. I bet she has her address too, although right now I'm not so sure I even want it. It's pretty obvious that my mother has no clue what this year has been like for me.

130

"So you must know where she is," I say at last.

"I don't. Honest. She didn't give me her address and I didn't ask for it. You have to let people do things at their own speed, in their own way, Sandra."

"But weren't you even curious?"

"Look, I learned not to get involved long ago, not unless I'm asked." I think about how Margie's life is a set of careful routines, work in the back office behind the key wall every day, Friday nights out at the Wa-Tika, a mud facial on Thursdays. I guess that's how she copes. Helping my mother get out and helping me get a job were big gestures for her. Could I really expect more?

"And what the hell should I do now?" I feel I'm on the verge of crying, but I don't want to cry in front of Margie. I bet Margie didn't even cry the day her marriage broke up. She probably just packed up her uniform, shook her marriage off, and carried on.

"I can't tell you that, Sandra. That's something you have to figure out yourself."

On the way back across the street I think of the only unexplored *X* on Yurek's map — Margie's place. In a strange way, my father hadn't been too far off.

Chapter 21

I shut my bedroom door, even though no one else is home, and crawl way under my covers. I need to be alone and cocooned before I read my mother's new phone number. Seeing my mother's handwriting gives me a shock. I trace the numbers with my finger without even reading them, as though some part of her is present in the ink.

I reread the number over and over, committing it to memory. The first three numbers suggest that her new place is in Outremont. Then I suddenly remember Margie on the bus one morning, telling me how much my mother loved that neighbourhood. Margie herself moved there when she got married. I guess it's kind of logical that my mother would head in that direction too. Maybe she's back working at Herzel's Leather Shop, if it's still there. And if Aaron's still working there, he might be chasing after her again. Maybe he never married, and now she's decided to give in to his flirtations. She isn't even technically too old to start a whole new family. Mr. Herzel would want his son to have a son to inherit the business. That would be one way for her to get settled. And it would explain why she seems to have completely forgotten about me.

In the morning, I take the 80 bus down Park Avenue and get off at Bernard. I turn right and walk a block to where Herzel's Leather Shop should be. I don't really think she'll be here. I mean, that all happened twenty years ago. I just can't think of any other starting point. But I soon discover that Herzel's Leather Shop doesn't even exist anymore. In its place is a fabric store. Rolls of brightly coloured material sit in the window, reflecting against the glass. I stand back and look up to the balcony where Aaron used to stand, trying to entice my mother. She was only a bit younger than I am now, at the time. When I push open the door a bell tinkles, luring a woman in a tangerine-coloured sari out of a doorway behind the counter. "Can I help you?" she says. She has a bright red dot on her forehead.

"Well, actually, I was wondering if you could tell me who lives upstairs," I say.

"Why do you want to know that?" she asks, knitting her brows.

"I'm just trying to find someone," I say.

"Well, you won't find them up there. My family lives there."

"Oh," I feel my heart sink. Did I really expect

to find her so easily? Then I have an idea. I pull out the picture of my mother doing the can-can. I may be crazy for showing this stranger such an old picture, but my instincts tell me that my mother might actually look like this again. Not her actual features, but her expression — that twirling, free, laughing expression. In any case, it's the only picture I have.

"Have you seen this woman around?" I ask, passing her the photo.

The woman looks a bit puzzled, but takes it and holds it close to her face. I'm encouraged that she doesn't say no outright. She even tilts the photo to the left and right. Then she looks at me closely, as though she's seeing my face in the picture. I guess I forgot that I do look a lot like my mother. Finally she turns her head and calls something out in a foreign language. A younger girl, about my age, comes out. I assume she is the woman's daughter. They are wearing identical saris. The mother passes her the picture and they look at it together. Occasionally, they look up at me. The younger girl finally says, "We're not sure, but it could be the woman who works across the street, at Nick's. It kind of looks like her." The girl points behind me. I turn to see a café where a large neon sign says "Nick's."

I walk to the front of the store, and look out over the rolls of silk, across the street and into the café. The wall facing me has huge windows, so it's easy to see inside. My mother is wearing an apron, tied over her jeans. She pulls a pad and pen out of its pocket and moves over to where a couple is sitting in a window seat. She writes down their order, scoops up their menus and turns to where a man — Nick, I assume — is sticking his head out of a hole in the wall. In my mind, I imagine her calling, "two eggs over easy hold the bacon."

Now what do I do? I can feel the Indian mother and daughter staring at me, boring holes into my back. Across the street is my waitress mother, serving breakfast to strangers. I can't exactly waltz into the restaurant, can I? "Hi Mom. I'll have an order of French toast please. You know how I like it." I never pictured our reunion happening in such a public place. I've got to get home. I've got to get over to Park and hop on the bus and take this piece of information home with me, to the empty flat, and think about what I'll do with it.

When my mother eventually disappears into the kitchen, I leave the store. I'm halfway to the corner when the daughter comes running after me.

"Here, you forgot this," she's calling, waving the picture in the air above her, making it look as though my mother is flying.

When she hands it to me, she smiles. It's a really forced I-know-how-you-must-be-feeling smile. Sure, how would she know? Her mother never left her.

Chapter 22

All that week, while my father's away, my mother's new phone number is stuck to the fridge with a ladybug magnet. Whenever I look at it the rhyme pops into my head — *ladybug, ladybug, fly away home, your house is on fire and your children are alone*. Well, the house isn't on fire, but I am alone. And if the house were on fire, there's no way my mother would even know. Not unless I called to tell her. Or popped in at Nick's.

I still haven't been able to take either of those steps. I keep picturing my mother in her waitress uniform. I couldn't see her expression too clearly from across the street, but she looked comfortable, like she'd been waitressing all her life. She seemed settled. I mean, she has a job and an apartment. What more could she be waiting for?

On Saturday, the day my father's coming home, I decide to cook a roast chicken for dinner. I put the small bird in the roasting pan and ring it with peeled potatoes, just like my mother used to. The snow is falling lightly outside, covering our streets in white just in time for Christmas. I think how the same snow is falling outside my mother's window somewhere in Outremont. I wonder what she'll do for Christmas this year. Will she just block it out, or will she make herself a tiny meal? Maybe she'll spend it serving turkey dinner specials to people who have no families, at Nick's.

Either way, she's bound to have a better Christmas than the one we had last year. Outside, the storefronts were covered in tinsel and streamers, crèches were buried in fake snow, and pine trees were lined up like bowling pins at the corner lot. But inside our house it could have been any time of year at all. Our fake tree never even came out of its box and my mother didn't bother making a turkey. She just bought some turkey pot pies.

Christmas day, Yurek came over at noon and he and my father disappeared soon afterwards. In the evening, when the pot pies and salad were ready, my mother knocked lightly on my door. It was just the two of us, sitting at the fake marble table. Then, suddenly, Yurek returned. He was surprised to discover that my father wasn't home yet. He asked us where we thought he might be and, for the first time in months, my mother laughed. I don't know what she found so funny, but I think it was the way Yurek suddenly wasn't in control of my father.

Later, my mother surprised me by pulling a red box out from under the sofa. I opened the lid slowly. Inside was something made of light blue silky material, wrapped in green tissue paper. I held up the straps and a full-length dress with a bow at the waist shimmered to the floor. It was for my grad, the one I never went to. My mother had to coax me down the hall to try it on. When I returned, she urged me to turn around, like a model. The silk swooshed against my legs as I spun. I never felt so pretty in my life. At that moment, Yurek sauntered down the hall. I felt his eyes taking me in. My mother must've too because she suddenly told me that that was enough — I should go take it off.

Suddenly, we heard a huge crash coming from the back of the flat. We all ran through the kitchen and into the shed. It was so cold, my skin goose-bumped immediately. The back door was frozen shut, as it always is in December. My mother just stood completely still, as if she'd frozen. Yurek ordered me to fetch some cups of hot water to melt the ice. The water turned to steam when it hit the metal bolts.

Finally, the door gave. Yurek tugged hard and in toppled my father, his body crumpled and covered in snow. Beyond him, in the moonlight, I saw his footprints in the waist-deep snow. Yurek carried him to his room while my mother and I sat on the sofa listening to the sounds of Yurek taking care of my drunk father behind the closed door. My mother shredded the tissue paper from my gift as she waited, letting it fall like grass onto her slippered feet.

My new dress would need to be dry cleaned and repaired. It was covered in dirt from the shed walls, as well as wet spots from the water. The bow, which must have caught on a hook, was torn in half.

In the morning, the shards of green paper still littered the carpet and the supper dishes hadn't moved from the table. I suppose I should have known then that my mother had crossed a line. She was so distant after that night, as if she hadn't thawed yet. It must have been soon after that she went across the street to ask Margie to help her escape. And all those times that I caught her just staring into her tea, when I assumed she was replaying Christmas night in her head, she was probably planning what to take, or picturing the room she'd soon be hiding out in.

I have set the table nicely, with the red Christmas tablecloth, and I even set out some red candles, although I don't know if I'll light them. I sit the pinecone-and-holly centrepiece between the candles and drape a string of tinsel around the kitchen window. Then I stand back and admire it. It looks nice. I'm not exactly sure why I'm going to all this trouble. My father and I haven't seen each other or spoken since the night he kicked Yurek out. Maybe this is my way of thanking him.

I had to go into the shed earlier to find the Christmas box. When I passed the trap door to the wine cellar, I thought about how I've never actually been down there. Sitting here now, waiting for the chicken to cook, I think how incredible it is that my mother lived in this house for almost two decades and never once set foot in it.

I put on my winter jacket and rummage through my father's workbench for a flashlight. Then I loop my finger into the ice-cold brass ring on the floor and pull the lid up, shining the light into the hole.

I descend slowly, clutching the sides of the ladder. At the bottom, I step gingerly onto the base, which is hard-packed earth covered in sawdust. I turn slowly, holding my flashlight out like a gun. The hole swells down here to a large bulb shape. In it are shelves stacked with wine bottles, a barrel with handles on the top, huge bottles encased in baskets and a small workbench with hoses hanging from hooks above it. Also above the workbench, held into the earth with rusty nails, are some pictures. When I look closely I see that they are of me, my mother, and my father. Most of them are yellowed and curled from the dampness of the cellar.

I see all three of us in summer clothes, my parents' arms around each other, me in the middle, trying to see them and the camera all at once so that my face is a blur, an ice cream melting in my hand. There is one of me on a horse, my father steadying me, his large hands around my waist, my mother smiling in the background. Another shows an older me standing near my mother at the foot of the maple tree, doing nothing, our arms hesitating toward each other. And the final picture is of my mother and father looking much younger, younger than I ever remember seeing them. They are in a rowboat. My father is at the oars, his back to the camera. My mother is leaning back, letting one hand trail in the choppy water. Her mouth is open in a wide laugh, a responsive laugh, as though my father has just said something witty. The boat is headed toward a dock that juts out into the picture. At its tip is a sign: Lachine Rapids Rowing Boats, One Dollar a Ride. The X near the water, I think.

I feel like an archeologist who has just discovered another secret tomb under the pyramids. These pictures are all testaments of the past, of happier times in my childhood, of happy times before I was even born. They are proof that my parents' life together wasn't always a disaster. It occurs to me that the picture of my mother doing the can-can belongs with these, and so does the picture of me that my mother must have carried around in her maid's uniform. They are both part of the same early story.

Back upstairs, I grab the pictures, along with the slip of paper bearing my mother's phone number. I descend the ladder far more surely this time. The cellar is familiar already, and my father was right all those years. There's nothing to be afraid of down here. I tack up my mother's new number, along with the two new pictures. Now the wall's complete.

As I climb back up to the shed, I think that if my father notices the new pictures, I'll know that he actually looks at the wall when he comes down here to fetch his wine. I hope he notices the change. I hope we haven't blended in, forgotten, with the dirt.

Chapter 23

The whole house is now filled with the delicious aroma of roasting chicken. I'm working on the salad, chopping lettuce, cucumbers, and tomatoes.

I hear my father's key in the front door just as I'm taking the bird out of the oven and transferring it to a large plate.

"Hello," he says, coming in to the kitchen. He doesn't exactly look me in the eyes when he says this, but at least he isn't studying the floor either.

"Hi," I respond. "I made a meal." It's a dumb thing to say, as if he's lost his senses.

"It smells good," he says hesitantly. It's the first time he's ever directly complimented my food.

I set the chicken and bowls of roasted potatoes and green salad on the table. My father takes two long-stemmed wine glasses off the shelf. Then he disappears into the shed. My heart pounds as I hear him pull up the cellar door and climb down the ladder. I can picture the bottles sitting on shelves to the right. But will he look left? Will he see the wall?

When he comes back up he says nothing. His face is inscrutable. I'm kind of disappointed but relieved at the same time. I had hoped he would notice the additions, but I also know that there will be lots of things to admit when he does. He opens the bottle and without even asking me if I want any, pours us each a glass of wine.

I watch the deep red liquid fill the glass, thinking how much conflict this wine has caused over the years. I can't believe I'm really about to taste it.

My father raises his glass toward me, and without looking at me directly, says "Cheers" under his breath. I lift my own glass and reach over the table to clink his. The tinkle of glass hitting glass is the most contact we've had in ages.

The wine is sweet. It tingles in my throat and warms my body. I want to say "Thanks, Dad," but I haven't called him Dad in so long, the word won't come.

"Thanks. It's good," I say instead. I sincerely mean this. The wine really is good. I wonder how it made my father feel all these years when my mother continually refused to taste it. "I've quit my job," I say at last, to break the silence. The little white lie won't hurt.

"Oh, why?"

"It was only temporary. I'm thinking of going back to school."

"That's good. You're smart," he says, totally

surprising me. I always thought my good marks meant nothing to him.

"I wanted to study more myself, but, you know, the war ..." My father's voice trails off. I don't know what to say. He doesn't usually talk to me about his past.

I cut us each a piece of the apple pie I bought yesterday at Jacques's and scoop some ice cream onto it. My father refills our wine glasses. He seems pleased that I'm enjoying it.

When he's done, my father reaches into his back pocket and pulls out a slip of paper. I recognize it immediately as my mother's phone number. He's staring at it as though he's conjuring up Anna's face behind the letters and numbers.

"How?" he asks, simply.

I tell him everything, about Margie's, the hotel, the emergency number, Nick's. Then the two of us just sit and stare out the window, past the yard that Siberia used to be caged up in, and over the snowy lane where the gray tin sheds cling to the backs of houses.

After a while, without saying a word, my father stands and retrieves an envelope from a pile of bills atop the fridge and hands it to me. For a minute, I think he might want me to pay the hydro bill, but then I see the word "Anna" on the envelope, in my father's strange German scrawl. I open it slowly, not knowing what to expect. Inside are some scraps of newspaper. I pull them out and there, in my hand, are a dozen cut-out copies of the ad —

"Anna, if you're out there, please come home."

I don't know what to say. I realize that what I'm holding in my hands is a huge confession.

"Why didn't you ever tell me, Dad?" I ask.

My father shrugs. "It wasn't working. I felt useless," he says.

"But why?"

"I don't know. Maybe because of things that happened long ago."

"What things?"

My father pauses before answering. "My sister," he says, taking a sip of wine.

"Your sister?" I wonder if he's going to tell me the story that Yurek tried to at the Wa-Tika, the one I didn't want to listen to.

My father pours himself more wine. "My mother told me to hide her if I heard soldiers. Once she was outside when they came. There wasn't time. One of them grabbed my sister and then another. They passed her back and forth like a ball." My father hesitates, then continues. "Then they dragged her downstairs. I could hear her crying. When my mother came home she was almost hysterical. I don't know what I could have done. I felt helpless. I felt that way again, when your mother left."

My arms are goosebumped. I can't believe my father had such an experience. I feel incredibly sorry for him. He must have felt guilty all his life for what happened to his sister.

"Did Mom know?"

"She couldn't listen to stories about my past. They disturbed her too much. It was a different world." I see the picture of my mother in the lineup of dancing girls, all kicking their feet up carelessly, laughing as though they hadn't a worry in the world. Yes, it would have been hard for her to relate.

My father is still holding the slip of paper, looking down at it intently. Then he slides it across the table to me. "I think you should call her. You're her daughter. She'll be glad to hear from you," he says.

I guess he's thinking how she probably wouldn't be glad to hear from him, not after the way he's been behaving for the past few years. Then he stares at his empty plate. I wonder who he's seeing there, his sister or his wife — the two women in his life that he let down. Two weeks ago, I would have added myself to that list, but now I'm not so sure.

I slide the copies of the ad across the table to my father. "You tried," I say. But I know that neither of us alone could have done anything. Maybe if we'd pooled our resources …

I lift the slip of paper with my mother's phone number.

Chapter 24

I dream of Siberia running through a vast field of deep snow, her strong legs lifting her gracefully over the powder. Her tongue hangs out and her blue eyes flash. She runs as though she is chasing an invisible ball, one that keeps bouncing ahead of her. At the distant edge of the field a gray stool appears, its long legs braced in the snow like a deer. I am seeing the scene as though I'm flying over Siberia toward the smudge of gray that darkens as we approach. As we near it, I realize it is the scene outside the cigarette stand in Kanawake, the stool and the old woman around whose feet Siberia was wrapped when we left her. The woman hunches over and stretches out her arm, pinching her fingers together the way you do when you want a dog to smell you. Siberia is leaping toward her, happy and free, her tail wagging even as she jumps. Then, suddenly, I am on the dog, riding her like a horse. I dig my hands deep into her fur to hang on.

Siberia leads us to the woman, never slowing down, even as we almost fly into her. Then she stops dead at the woman's feet. The woman straightens up and laughs, a loud laugh that flies out across the vast landscape we have just come from. The laugh has colour and it paints the sky a lacy pink. The woman's head is so far back I can't see her face, which is hooded by a parka. I want her to stop laughing so I can see her, and so I pull on the string of the hood. It works and she immediately stops laughing and looks down. Then she reaches out again, her palm flat this time. I think she wants to pet Siberia's face, but it is my face that she strokes instead.

"Such a pity," she says. "It was always such a pity about that dog. You did the right thing."

I drop down to my knees in the snow. The old woman's face is the face of my mother.

The image tears me awake, then fades, even as I try to hang on to it. Then I remember with a start that today is the day of my mother's visit. I can't believe I slept at all, never mind dreamed. And why did I dream of Siberia? I haven't thought about her for ages. I'm sure Siberia's not the first thing my mother and I are going to talk about. It's not like I'm going to walk her down the hall, show her the yard next door and ask if she knows what's missing, like some sort of guessing game.

As I'm dressing, I wonder how the visit will go. I mean, how do you receive your own mother that you haven't seen for a year into her old house? Do you serve her tea like a guest? Do you show her to a chair? Do you offer to take her coat and hang it up?

Or, do you simply open the door and stand back and assume that she'll just walk right in and reclaim her territory? Lady of the house once again?

The fearful thought enters my mind, snapping it like a dry twig, that she may feel like Siberia would if she had been found and led back into her pen. Maybe that's the message my dream was sending me. That she's coming reluctantly. That she wants to retain her new-found freedom. She'll stand at the threshold of her former home, the one she couldn't stand to live in anymore, and freeze. I picture my father and I having to lead her like a blind person down the hall.

And how will we make conversation? Is it going to be question-and-answer format, like a trial. And who will ask the questions? It's not as clear-cut as in a court case, where there's a victim and a criminal. We're all kind of mixed up together.

Our conversation on the phone yesterday was hard enough. She was totally surprised to hear from me. Maybe she thought she never would, not unless there was some huge emergency worth calling about. I didn't say half the things I thought I was going to say. I thought I wanted her to know how hard the past year has been for me. I thought I wanted her to accept some responsibility for that, but I became kind of tongue-tied, just like her. She did say she was glad I'd called, that she had wanted to call herself, so many times. But I cut her short on that one. I'm not going to listen to any excuses. Then I invited her over. I didn't beg, I just asked. When I hung up my hands were sweaty and my heart was pounding. I could hear my father rinsing dishes in the sink. I felt as though the water was roaring in my head like a waterfall. I wanted to hide away and never face her after that.

But hiding isn't an option. There's been too much of that around here already. I can see Danny tucking himself in the corner of the boxcar, or hiding out in an empty hotel room picking dirt from his nails, anything to avoid having to do something with his life. And that's what my father does, only he hides out in his wine cellar when life gets tough. And now I know my mother was living in room 701 like some kind of fugitive, hiding from her messed-up marriage. And now she's hiding in her new flat somewhere, wanting to call me, but unable to.

And what about me? Have I been hiding too? Is that what my job was, an opportunity to hide, to avoid facing my future? I mean, shouldn't I be doing something better with my life?

Right now, we're doing a quick cleanup. I can hear the vacuum cleaner running in the living room and I promised to freshen up the bathroom. It's like we want the house to be perfect, to show her that we've put in some effort. As if we're the ones who need to make amends, who need to get things right, even though she's the one who disappeared. And who knows? Maybe we are.

My father is actually washing windows, polishing off the grime to let in more of the winter light. And I notice, as I fill a bucket of soapy water to begin cleaning the bathroom, that the hook and eye have finally been fixed and are now solidly fastened to the wood. And the tap in the sink has stopped dripping. I think I understand why he's making all these little gestures.

Last night, after my father went to bed, I climbed down into his wine cellar and stared at the picture wall. It occurred to me that the images shouldn't be left to rot down there in the damp hole. They needed to be brought up into the light. So, that's what I did. I arranged them kind of haphazardly on the fridge with various magnets. I figure that if my mother's taking in her surroundings with a keen eye, she'll notice them. They should surprise her, especially the one of me that she once carried around in her apron pocket at the hotel. The other one that might stump her is the one of her and her pals doing the can-can. As for the others, I'm not sure she ever knew that my father kept these pictures tacked to his cellar wall.

But it's probably about time she did.

The doorbell rings, its high note reverberating through the long flat. My father's in the kitchen, which means I am closest to the door. I start down the hallway. The steps I take seem to be in slow motion. I can see my mother's silhouette against the front door curtain, the sunlight behind her, as though she's a shadow puppet.

My hand reaches out to turn the doorknob, but it doesn't seem like my hand, as if it's disconnected from my body.

In my mind, all I can think is that I still don't know if I can forgive her. I feel cold, as if I'm back in the cellar.

Then I open the door and see her. At first, it's like I'm looking at a photograph. Her features are frozen on paper: hazel eyes, red hair, half-smile.

But then she moves. Her hand is reaching out toward me.

My mind is blank, except for one thought. She is my mother. And she is here. And that seems like a really good place to start.